"Earth to Jan

She looked up into concerned face. O she'd stopped righ blocking traffic.

"What's wrong?" he asked.

"I don't know. I—I think I remembered something. But it was more like a feeling than an actual memory."

"What did it feel like?"

"I felt…*alone.*"

"You're not alone."

"Not yet."

If she saw a flash of guilt in his eyes, it was gone almost instantly. "Let's go inside."

They stepped through the automatic door, and she once again felt that sudden and brief surge of adrenaline.

"I think I remember being here," she said, excitement and hope erupting inside her like a geyser. Maybe it would all start to come back now. Maybe this nightmare was almost over.

Or maybe it was only beginning.

Running on Empty

MICHELLE CELMER

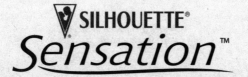

SILHOUETTE®
Sensation™

First published in Great Britain 2005
Silhouette Books, Eton House, 18-24 Paradise Road,
Richmond, Surrey TW9 1SR

© Michelle Celmer 2005

ISBN 0 373 27413 0

18-1105

Printed and bound in Spain
by Litografía Rosés S.A., Barcelona

MICHELLE CELMER

lives in southeastern Michigan with her husband, their three children, two dogs and two cats. When she's not writing or busy being a mum, you can find her in the garden or curled up with a romance novel. And if you twist her arm real hard, you can usually persuade her into a day of power shopping.

Michelle loves to hear from readers. Visit her website at www.michellecelmer.com, or write to her at PO Box 300, Clawson, MI 48017, USA.

For Steve

Prologue

It would be so easy to kill her.

So easy to wrap his hands around her neck and squeeze until the life drained from her body. To plant the barrel of his gun to her temple and pull the trigger.

Only that wasn't part of the game.

He liked to see them suffer. To know that for the rest of their lives they would live in fear. Fear of him. And this one, she would suffer. She would learn her place. She stuck her nose in where it didn't belong, took what was rightfully his.

But when he got what he was looking for, when he no longer needed her and the game was over, she would pay.

With her life.

Chapter 1

Running across a body in a cordoned-off crime scene was rare enough in a community the size of Twin Oaks, but the odds of running *over* one in the toy department of the local Save Mart had to be about a million to one.

Making this his lucky day.

Cursing a blue streak, Detective Mitch Thompson swerved his cart and narrowly missed rolling over a denim-clad leg. The woman lay sprawled on her back, looking, as far as he could tell, unharmed. And breathing. She was definitely pulling in a sufficient amount of air. He crouched down beside her and pressed two fingers to her throat, finding a strong pulse.

Okay, so what was the deal?

He tapped her cheek lightly, finding her skin warm and soft beneath his fingers. "Ma'am, can you hear me?"

She didn't respond. Then he noticed the blood. It soaked through the back of her hair, transforming it from honey-colored to crimson.

Well, that would explain it. Damn, he really didn't need this tonight. He pulled out his cell phone and dialed 911. He gave the operator his badge number and the location of the store. "I have a woman down, twenty-five to thirty years old, with a head injury."

After the operator assured him help was on the way, he disconnected and shoved the phone back into his pocket. Thinking she might have passed out and hit her head on the way down, he unzipped her jacket to look for a medic-alert necklace, searched her wrists, shoving up one sleeve, then the other. No bracelets, no rings. Nothing to indicate a chronic medical condition.

He noticed bruises forming on her forearms and elbows. Odd, considering she was flat on her back. When a person fell backward, they didn't typically land on their arms. Could she have fallen forward and rolled over?

The pool of blood under her head began to spread, and though he didn't want to move her, he had to stop the bleeding. He searched his pockets for something to press against the wound but came up empty. Out of desperation, he grabbed a beanbag animal from the bin above him and eased it under her head, doing his best not to move her neck. He doubted it was sterile, but it would have to suffice.

"Ma'am, can you hear me?" he tried again. "Open your eyes."

She mumbled something incoherent.

He scanned the area for a purse or wallet, something

to identify her. He checked the pockets of her jacket, finding a few wadded tissues in one, a folded receipt with no store name on it in the other. He was about to check the pockets of her jeans when he heard a gasp behind him.

"What did you do to her?" A young girl with a nametag identifying her as Becky stood several feet away, gaping at the scene on the floor. Her eyes locked on the blood and all the color leeched from her face. The plastic basket of items she was holding clattered to the floor.

"Twin Oaks Police," he said, producing his badge.

She slapped a hand over her mouth, asking through her fingers, "Is she d-dead?"

"No, Becky, but I need to get her to a hospital." And he needed to get the clerk moving before he had two unconscious, bleeding women on his hands. "Go to the front entrance and flag down the emergency personnel when they pull up and lead them back to me. Can you do that?"

"S-sure." She backed up a few steps, eyes riveted on the woman, then turned and scurried away.

He stuck his badge back in his jacket and yawned so deeply his eyes teared. Christ, he was tired. He should be home in bed right now. It was after midnight, which meant it was Saturday and officially his day off. If he hadn't let his sister Lisa talk him into stopping at the store for her, in bed is where he would probably be.

It had been a long, hellish week that resulted in the arrest of a man allegedly responsible for the brutal rape of five women. Mitch's arrest, thanks to an anonymous tip. Now all he wanted—what he desperately needed—was a few days off. God knows he'd earned it. Between work and helping care for their mother while she recovered from back surgery, he was running himself ragged. After he dropped the groceries off he had planned to go home, unplug the phone, crawl into bed and sleep straight through until Sunday. Now he'd have to go into the station and file a report.

The woman on the floor moaned, wincing when she tried to move her head.

"Ma'am, can you hear me? You need to lie still. Help is on the way." He braced one hand under her head and cupped the other over her cheek to hold her immobile. Her delicately boned face felt fragile and looked small cradled in his palm.

She reached up in a vain attempt to pry his hand away. "Hurts."

"I know it hurts, but you could make it worse by moving."

Her lids fluttered open and she looked up at him, eyes unfocused and bleary—eyes a spectrum of speckled gray, like the stones he used to collect on the beach at Lake Superior when he was a kid. For several seconds, he found himself suspended in their depths.

"Please," she murmured. "Please, don't let him—" She grimaced, as if the effort to speak was too painful. Her eyes rolled up, and he could tell she was sinking back into unconsciousness.

"Don't let him what?" he urged. "Did someone hurt you?"

In a surprising burst of strength, she reached out and

clutched the front of his leather jacket, her eyes clear and wild with fear. "Don't let him kill me."

Mitch watched, feeling an uncharacteristic surge of empathy as the paramedics wheeled the woman away. She looked so small and helpless on the gurney, her skin ashen in contrast to the stark white bandages on the gash at the base of her skull. Since those brief seconds when she'd pleaded for her life, she hadn't regained consciousness, but her single utterance told him everything he needed to know to get an investigation started.

This had been no accident.

As a result, the store was crawling with Twin Oaks' finest. If the suspect was ballsy enough to attack a woman in a well-lit store, who knew what else he might be capable of.

"Detective?"

Mitch turned to Officer Greene, one of the uniforms dispatched to the scene. Greene was new to the force, six months out of the academy, but what he lacked in experience he made up for in enthusiasm. He reminded Mitch of himself ten years ago. "Find anything?"

"We combed the area but we didn't find a purse or anything else that might identify her. We've got two men searching the parking lot, and another two in the alley, in case the perp slipped out the back."

"What about her cart?"

He nodded to the left. "At the end of the aisle. No purse or any identification."

Mitch followed him to the cart abandoned a few feet from where he'd found the victim.

"Looks like she was on a budget," Greene said.

The cart contained generic brand vegetables by the case—six of them altogether. There were also diapers and disposable wipes, and a couple dozen jars of baby food. It would be a safe bet that their Jane Doe had a family, although she hadn't been wearing a wedding ring. Divorced maybe? A single mother? Or maybe she just happened to take her jewelry off and had forgotten to put it back on when she left the house.

Sighing, he dragged a hand through his hair and massaged away the knots from the back of his neck. "There are probably a couple kids out there wondering why Mommy hasn't come home yet."

"How bad was she?"

"Blunt force trauma to the back of the head. Too severe to be from a fall. From the bruising on her arms, I'm guessing she was hit from behind and thrown forward, then rolled over onto her back." He gestured to the tinted dome overhead that housed a security camera. "What about surveillance?"

"The store is old, so it's not exactly a state-of-the-art system. Picture quality couldn't be much worse. Maybe if the victim knows him, she could identify him from the tapes."

Her words echoed in his head—*don't let him kill me.* She could still be in danger. They needed to find out who she was and if she knew who had done this to her. *They* meaning *him.* Which also meant that sleep would have to wait. Though he wasn't sure why, he didn't trust this case to anyone else. It was as if, in those few seconds she'd looked up at him, they'd bonded somehow.

Bonded? Christ, he must be delirious from exhaustion. If he told anyone at the station his theory, they would tell him he needed his head examined.

"Make sure someone takes down the plates of all the cars in the lot," he told Greene. "With all this food, I doubt she was walking."

Greene followed him to his cart. "It's a good thing you found her. Who knows how long she would have lain there bleeding. The store is practically deserted this time of night."

"Yeah, my lucky day." Not.

"You seem to be having a lot of those lately. That was some arrest. Did you get a confession?" Greene had what could only be described as hero worship in his eyes.

Mitch didn't deserve the recognition. He'd been completely stumped until an anonymous letter had been dropped on his desk. It named the suspect, gave his address, and even disclosed where the evidence—trinkets taken from each of the victims—could be found. The entire arrest had been unbelievably easy.

Too easy.

"The interrogation went on for twelve hours and he didn't crack," Mitch said. "But the D.A. thinks we have enough physical evidence to convict."

"This your stuff?" Greene asked, motioning to his groceries.

"Yeah." Mitch glanced down at his cart. No time to pay for it now. Besides, the death-by-chocolate ice cream was oozing out and creating a brown puddle on the floor. He'd just have to stop somewhere on the way home, which by the looks of things, wouldn't be until morning.

Greene gestured to the basket the employee had dropped. "What about that stuff?"

"It's not part of the crime scene. You find anything else, page me."

"Where are you headed?"

"I'm going over to the hospital to get an ID on her," Mitch said. "With any luck, I'll have this case wrapped up by morning."

Pain, sharp and relentless, lanced the back of her head, pounded through her brain like a jackhammer and wrapped itself around her eyeballs. She tried to lift her lids, but piercing white light seared her retinas.

"That's it," a voice said. It sounded distant, muffled. "Open your eyes."

"Too bright," she muttered, nearly choking on her own words. Her mouth felt funny, as if it had been stuffed with cotton.

"Why don't we try sitting you up a little." There was a humming sound, and she felt herself rising, as if some invisible force held her suspended in midair. Maybe she was dead. There had been a bright light.

Nah. Heaven wouldn't smell like rubbing alcohol. And it wouldn't be so loud. All around her she heard the drone of muffled voices, odd beeps and bleeps, the thud of footsteps. Did people in heaven even have feet?

She tried to swallow, but her tongue felt thick and sticky. "Water?" she croaked, her voice sounding coarse and unfamiliar.

A straw touched her lips but she sucked a bit too enthusiastically. The shock of the cold liquid made her gag and choke. Water spewed from her mouth and dribbled down her chin.

That must have been attractive. When she was able to speak, she would have to apologize to whoever it was she'd just sprayed. With caution, she forced her lids open, blinking several times to clear her vision, and found herself gazing into a pair of deep-set, chocolate brown eyes.

"Want to try that again?" he asked, holding up a plastic cup. His deep voice enfolded her like soft flannel, and any apprehension she'd been feeling melted away.

Entranced, she nodded and he lifted the cup, holding the straw to her lips.

"Take it slow this time."

She sucked in a few drops, rolling it around on her tongue before letting it slide down her throat. Much better. She sipped slowly on the straw, and all the while he kept those dark, watchful eyes trained on her. When she'd had enough, he set the cup on the tray beside her bed.

Bed? The haze in her peripheral vision cleared and her surroundings came into focus. "Where am I?"

"In the hospital. You were attacked. Do you remember what happened?"

"Attacked?" She tried to lean forward and was stopped short by a stab of pain at the base of her skull. She winced, squeezing her lids together.

He curled one large hand over her shoulder and pressed her back against the mattress. "Relax, you've got a pretty good lump on the back of your head."

That would explain the excruciating pain. She reached up to touch it, but tangled herself in her IV lines instead.

"Here, let me." Though his voice held a note of irritation and his eyes mirrored the emotion, his touch was undeniably gentle as he unwrapped the tubes from her fingers. When she was free, she reached up, grazing the small bandage taped to the back of her head. Considering the pain, she'd expected to find half her skull gone. This didn't seem so bad.

"Did you see who hit you?"

She shook her head, regretting the move instantly, as another wave of nauseating pain swept through her. "I don't remember being hit."

His face grim, he perched on the edge of her bed, and produced a small notepad out of the dark leather jacket he wore. Everything about him was dark. Dark clothes, dark hair, dark eyes. Even his expression was dark. "You were found with no identification. If you give me your name and number I'll call your family."

She must have looked confused, because he added, "I'm Detective Mitch Thompson. Twin Oaks P.D."

"Twin Oaks?" she asked and he flashed her a badge. Twin Oaks, Michigan. Why didn't that sound familiar?

"If you'll just give me your name."

"My name?"

"Yes, your name," he said. "I need to contact your family. They're probably worried about you."

"Right." Her family would be worried, wouldn't they? She opened her mouth to speak, but nothing happened. No name popped out.

She tried again, but still, nothing.

She looked down at the band on her wrist. *Jane Doe.* No, that wasn't right. She swallowed hard, a cold, itchy panic churning her belly. She tried again to summon a name, a mental picture of herself, but there was nothing there. No names, no familiar faces. No family.

Nothing.

This was all wrong. She clutched the thin blanket, willing her brain to work harder, to concentrate past the frantic thumping of her heart. The rush of blood echoed in her ears like static on a radio. If she could just turn the dial, adjust the frequency…

But there was nothing. It was as if a hole had been punched in her memory and her identity had just… leaked out.

"Are you okay?" Detective Thompson was on his feet. "Maybe I should get a doctor."

She thrust her arm out, clutching the sleeve of his jacket, oblivious to the pain the action induced. He was the only thing familiar, the only thing that felt real. "Don't leave me alone."

"Relax." He eased himself down, covering her hand with his own, prying it from his sleeve. His hand was warm and soft, comforting to the smallest degree. "If you tell me who you are, I can call your family."

"Family?" The panic rose, filling her throat with bile and gagging her. She couldn't speak, couldn't think. Did she have a family? Wouldn't she remember them?

A frown darkened his face even more. "Who are you afraid of? Did someone you know hurt you?"

Someone she knew? But, she didn't know *anyone*.

"Do you know who did this? Don't be afraid. I can protect you."

"I—I can't tell you," she said. Hearing the words, in

a voice so foreign it should have belonged to a stranger, sent an icy chill up her spine. Bile surged up, until she had to fight to keep it down.

"Why can't you tell me?"

"Because, I—I don't know who I am."

Chapter 2

Mitch pulled on the hospital scrubs the nurse had given him and shoved his soiled clothes into a plastic bag. In the span of about four hours he'd been bled on, spit on and puked on. It was all a part of the job, although he didn't typically encounter such a variety of bodily functions in one night. And he still had no identity on Jane Doe or the slightest clue who attacked her. No evidence had been found at the crime scene and no one shopping or working in the store had seen or heard a thing. As Greene had predicted, the security tape quality was very poor so they doubted a positive ID would be possible. It didn't look like the victim was going to be much help, either.

He strapped on his holster and shrugged into his jacket.

With a weary sigh, he pushed open the bathroom door and walked back to Jane Doe's cubicle. The doctor in charge of her care stood beside the bed checking her pulse. She was asleep now, probably all worn out from that *Exorcist* routine she'd pulled earlier.

The doctor checked her IV then motioned for Mitch to follow him, sliding the curtain closed on his way out.

"So," Mitch asked. "How is she?"

"Mild concussion. We'd like to keep her overnight, just in case."

"And the amnesia?"

"Temporary, I'm sure. The blow to the head wasn't that severe. Her memory loss was probably brought on by the psychological trauma. It could last days or weeks. Typically something will trigger a memory, a familiar name or face. I don't think she'll suffer any permanent damage."

"Could she be faking it?"

"Of course it's possible. There is something I'd like to show you." He led Mitch past the nurses' station to a wall of X rays. "Due to the nature of her injuries, we checked for possible skull fractures and broken bones in the arms and hands."

Mitch gazed up at the films spanning half the wall. "What am I looking for?"

"See these?" He indicated several areas in the X ray. "They're healed fractures. I counted seven altogether. Two in the skull, four fingers, her right arm. She also has an appendectomy scar, so I had films taken of her torso, as well."

"She had her appendix removed?"

He led him down to another set of films. "That, and I found four healed rib fractures. I didn't X-ray the legs, so there could be more."

"Christ." Gazing up at the films, he shook his head, disgust roiling his stomach. It looked as if someone had used her as a punching bag. "Can you tell when they happened?"

"I would guess that they all occurred after the bones were fully developed."

"Could it be from some kind of accident?"

"Unlikely. You can see in the fingers here that the bone was never set properly. For most of these injuries, I'd guess she was never seen by a doctor. It looks to me like a classic case of domestic abuse."

Mitch scrubbed a hand across his rough jaw. He'd seen the aftermath of domestic abuse as a patrolman and a detective, and it turned his stomach every time. Only now, as he pictured Jane Doe looking so fragile, IV lines crisscrossing the head of the bed, her silvery eyes wide and trusting, the sensation multiplied.

However, as innocent as those eyes appeared, the cop in him had to consider the possibility that she didn't really have amnesia. That she was hiding from someone. "If she was treated here for her injuries, could that be traced?"

The doctor nodded. "I thought of that, too. I've got someone working on it. But if it is abuse, odds are the abuser wouldn't bring her to the same hospital every time. It would begin to look suspicious."

"Look into it anyway. We may need the information to identify her." In his jacket pocket his phone began to ring. He thanked the doctor for his help and headed for the emergency room doors, checking the digital display. It was someone from the precinct.

"Thompson," Mitch answered.

"It's Greene. So far we've got nothing useable from security, but it'll take some time to go over all the tapes. We never found a purse or car and there were a couple thousand sets of prints in the general area. Basically, we got nada."

"Keep checking the security tapes," Mitch said. "Maybe we'll get a break."

"Any luck getting an ID on Jane Doe?"

"Not yet. She's got some kind of temporary amnesia." He leaned against the brick wall outside the emergency room door, his body sagging with fatigue. Through gritty, tired eyes, he could see the faintest glow of dawn shimmering on the horizon. He looked at his watch. It was now officially twenty-three hours since he'd dragged himself out of bed. "I'm going to hang out here until she wakes up and see if any of her memory has come back. When the hospital releases her I'll bring her by the precinct for prints. Maybe she's in the database."

"And if she's not? What will you do then?"

"I'm supposed to be off this weekend. If nothing pans out by then, she'll officially be someone else's problem.

Detective Thompson looked like a different man when he slept. The sharp planes of his face softened and he lost that look of quiet intensity that both soothed and unsettled her. He dozed in the chair by her window, his head propped in one big hand, long thick lashes fanning out across his cheeks.

Jane lay watching him, memorizing his features, for fear that the next time she closed her eyes he would vanish from her memory. Vaguely she recalled being moved to a private room. She still felt a little groggy and slightly disoriented and her head ached something fierce. All things considered though, she didn't seem to have been too badly damaged. Not physically, anyway. It would be awfully nice to know her own name, to know where she lived. She didn't like being trapped here in the hospital, playing the role of the victim. Somewhere, deep down, she knew she wasn't accustomed to feeling this way, and at the same time, it was hauntingly familiar.

This is temporary, she reminded herself. The doctor said her memory would return soon and she would be good as new.

From the chair across the room, Detective Thompson stirred. His eyes opened, focused on her, and he sat up. "You're awake."

"More or less. I'm feeling a little woozy." She rolled onto her side, propping herself up on one elbow. The detective was cute in the morning, in a rough, disheveled sort of way. Thick beard stubble shadowed his jaw and his voice had a husky quality that sent shivers down her spine. And the way he looked at her was so measured and deliberate. Like he could read her thoughts. Which at this point wouldn't get him far. There wasn't much left up there to think about. "You were here all night?"

He looked up, squinting against the sunlight pouring

in the window, then down at his watch. "Looks that way. I didn't mean to fall asleep."

He yawned and stretched, the green hospital scrubs he wore pulling taut across his chest and biceps. They didn't burst at the seams from hulking muscle mass. He was more the slim and athletic type. She couldn't say with any certainty if he was the type of man she was normally attracted to, but from where she sat now, she wouldn't kick him out of bed for getting crumbs on the sheets.

It occurred to her suddenly that he was dressed like a doctor—save for the holster and gun strapped at his side—and she wondered what happened to the clothes he'd been wearing. Then she recalled, with a stark clarity that made her cringe, what she'd done. "Sorry about your clothes," she said. "It wasn't one of my finer moments."

One eyebrow quirked up. "No?"

"At least, I don't think it was." She paused, chewing her lower lip.

"You still don't remember who you are?"

She shook her head, noting that the action didn't induce the same paralyzing pain as before. It had since reduced to a persistent, dull ache. The nausea had ebbed, as well and she actually felt hungry. "I think I may have also, um, spit water at you."

"You bled on me, too. But I won't hold it against you." A grin teased the corner of his mouth. It wasn't even a real smile and her stomach still did a half-gainer straight down to her toes. Was he trying to look adorable, or did it just come naturally?

"What else do you remember?" he asked.

"I remember waking up in the hospital."

"That's it?"

"Everything before that is gone. It's the weirdest feeling, like opening a book and finding blank pages. I know something is supposed to be there, but it's as if all the words are written in invisible ink." She sat up, pulling the light blanket up to her neck, feeling self-conscious in the flimsy hospital gown. "Where are my clothes?"

"I think there's a bag of stuff in the drawer next to the bed. You didn't have a purse or any identification when I found you."

She slid the drawer open and found a plastic bag marked "personal belongings." "I don't suppose you know when they're letting me out of here."

"Today, I think. Why? You've got plans?"

She swore she detected a note of suspicion in his voice. "We have to try and find out who I am, don't we?"

"We?"

"Yeah, *we*. I assume you're the one investigating my attack. I'm not going to sit around doing nothing. I want to help."

"Ms.—"

"Don't tell me that put in the same situation you would want to sit around twiddling your thumbs, waiting for your memory to magically reappear."

"No, I wouldn't, but—"

"The doctor told me that seeing something familiar could trigger a memory. It only makes sense that I get out and try to find something familiar. If I have to, I'll do it alone."

"I wouldn't advise that," Detective Thompson said. "You have no money, no identification, no transportation. And we have no idea who attacked you, or why."

"You think I'm in danger?"

"I'm not ready to make any assumptions at this point." He sighed, leaning forward and raking a hand through his tousled hair. Hair the same warm brown as his eyes and just long enough to cover the tops of his ears and brush the collar of his jacket. And soft looking. She imagined what it would feel like to run her fingers through it.

Oh, yeah, like that would ever happen. He was probably married. Or at least attached. For that matter, maybe she was, too.

"So when do we start?" she asked.

"*We* don't do anything. First off, I don't even know if I'll be the one investigating. And second, I don't make it a habit of dragging victims along with me while I work a case."

"*My* case. Also, there's the slight problem of me not knowing where I live. Where do you plan to put me?"

"A halfway house. You should be safe there until we figure out who you are and who did this. As long as you stay put," he added.

No way. No way was he dumping her off at some crummy halfway house. If he expected her to agree to that, he was in for a big surprise. "But the sooner I get my memory back, the sooner you solve the case, right?"

"You can call the precinct if you remember anything."

Was he joking? Did he honestly expect her to sit around doing *nothing?*

Fat chance.

She dug through the clothes bag, wondering how something that belonged to her could look so completely foreign. "They're all cut up," she said, pulling out a mutilated pair of jeans and T-shirt. The only thing left intact was a dark blue jacket.

"They cut your clothes off in the E.R. It's standard procedure."

She looked up at him, aghast. "What am I supposed to do, walk out of here *naked?*"

"I'm sure the hospital will give you some clothes, and the halfway house will have things for you." Detective Thompson stood, pulling his jacket on. "I'm going to try to find the doctor to see when they're letting you out of here, then I'm going to make a few phone calls and set things up."

She was pretty sure, from the determined set of his jaw, that arguing would get her nowhere, so she nodded. She'd think of something, some way to make him see things her way. And if that didn't work, she'd have to take matters into her own hands. She had rights. He couldn't force her to do anything she didn't want to do.

She stuffed the jeans and shirt in the bag and looked the jacket over. Searching the pockets, she found wadded tissues in one and a faded receipt in the other. There was no store name, just a few random numbers. Then she turned it over to check the other side and gasped at the note scrawled there.

Detective Thompson stopped halfway to the door. "What's wrong?"

"Did you put this in my jacket?" she asked, holding the paper up.

"No. Is it familiar?"

"Sort of," she said, holding it out to him. On the back of the receipt written very lightly in pencil was a name: Detective Mitch Tompson.

Chapter 3

"This doesn't make any sense," Mitch said. "What are you doing with my name in your pocket?"

She shrugged, looking equally baffled. "How should I know? Have we met?"

No, a man didn't forget a woman like her. The wide, silvery eyes alone were enough to snag his attention. Had he met her in a social situation he would have noticed, and he'd have been interested. "I'm sure we haven't. I would have remembered."

"Maybe the person who hit me stuck it in there."

"I know a good way to find out." He pulled a pen and notepad out of his jacket, opening it to a blank page. He handed them both to her. "Write my name."

She penned his name across the paper and handed it back to him. After comparing the two, there was no doubt in his mind. They were identical. She'd even left the *h* out of his last name both times.

"It was definitely you," he said, holding it up for her to see. "But why?"

She shrugged, looking genuinely bewildered.

Damn. What had started out as a simple attack had just become a lot more complicated.

It couldn't be a coincidence that they'd been in the same store and she had his name. It also meant he wouldn't be passing this case off to anyone. Not until he knew why and how he was involved. Not after the last time he found himself involved in a case. That had nearly cost him his career.

So much for his weekend off.

In his pocket, his pager vibrated. He pulled it out and checked the display. "I have to make a call," he told her. "Don't go anywhere."

"What, I'm gonna sneak away with my rear end hanging out the back of my gown?" she called after him.

With an amused shake of his head, he headed to the elevator bay, where he could safely use his cell phone. She didn't pull any punches. He had to admire her for that. And he couldn't deny that he liked her. So why did he feel this impending sense of doom?

Maybe he liked her *too* much. He felt an urge to protect and shelter her that he didn't typically get. Well, not since…a long time ago.

Shrugging off the unpleasant memory, he dialed the precinct.

"We've got your guy on the security tape following the victim through the store," Greene said. "He's wearing a hooded jacket, so we can't get a look at his face and the picture quality sucks. Maybe the victim will recognize him."

It was a long shot. Seeing her attacker might be enough to snap her out of it. "I'll bring her by as soon as they discharge her. If she can't ID him from the tape, we can sit her down with the mug books."

"I'm off in five minutes. I'll leave everything with Marco."

Mitch called halfway houses next, until he found her a vacant room. It wouldn't be the Marriott, but it would be safe enough until someone claimed her. With any luck, her memory would return after watching the tape and he'd be taking her home instead.

When he got back to her room, the doctor was there.

Ms. Doe looked up at him and smiled, and it washed over him like sunshine. Ribbons of golden hair fanned out across the pillow framing her delicate face like a halo. Her skin was milky white and smooth—fragile looking, like the porcelain figurines his mother collected. He recalled how soft her skin had felt against his fingers when he'd touched her face back in the store. The sudden, intense pull of lust the memory evoked nearly floored him.

What the hell was he doing? *Fantasizing* about her? Real smart, Mitch. Like she didn't already have enough problems.

His pager vibrated and he wasn't surprised to see that it was his sister. She would hound him relentlessly until he picked up her groceries. He erased the number and stuck it back in his pocket.

"They're cutting me loose," Jane said. "I'm a free woman."

"I'll sign her release and have the nurse find her some clothes," the doctor said. "She'll need to come back in a week to have the stitches removed."

"And the amnesia?" Mitch asked. "Can you do anything for that?"

"Give it a little time. Try taking her back to the scene of her attack if she's comfortable with that. When she's ready to deal with the incident, I think her memory will come back on it's own."

"But you think she should try to find something familiar?"

"As long as she's okay with that, I think it's a good idea," the doctor said.

Ms. Doe shot Mitch an I-told-you-so look. Christ, she had attitude. She was going to be a major pain in the behind, he could just tell.

"And if her memory doesn't come back?" Mitch asked.

"If her condition hasn't improved in a week we'll schedule an appointment with a neurologist." The doctor hooked her chart on the foot of the bed. "Ibuprofen every four to six hours should ease any discomfort."

"I'll be right back," Mitch told her, and followed the doctor into the hall. "Did you find anyone with injuries matching hers?"

"Not yet. It could take a day or two."

Mitch pulled a business card out of his jacket pocket. "Call me if you find anything."

When he stepped back into the room, Ms. Doe was out of bed, her back to him, gazing out the window. Her height surprised him. Based on tenacity alone, he'd expected her to be taller. He guessed now that the top of her head would barely reach his chin. She was slight, delicate-looking even, until she opened her mouth and all of that attitude spilled out. It was obvious, if it weren't for the amnesia—assuming she really did have it—she was the kind of woman who looked out for herself.

It was hard to imagine someone physically abusing her—or her allowing it.

She leaned forward to look out the window, the edges of her gown pulling open and—*whoa!* He got an eyeful of smooth, rounded, ivory flesh. Something hot and carnal flickered to life inside of him. Something he hadn't let himself feel in an awfully long time. Apparently, too long. Try as he might, he had a hell of a time looking away.

He forced himself to speak. "Recognize anything?"

She spun around, startled. As if realizing the view she'd just given him, she reached back to hold her gown closed. "No, I don't. And I just want to say for the record, I don't appreciate you talking about me behind my back."

He folded his arms over his chest and leaned against the doorjamb. "Who says we were talking about you?"

"Oh, please. I have amnesia, I'm not brain-dead. Who else would you be talking about? If you have information about me, I want to hear it. I may remember something."

There were certain things he didn't really want to tell her yet, things he wasn't sure she was ready to hear, but she was right, anything could trigger a memory. "We were talking about healed injuries he found in your X rays."

She frowned, her pale brows pulling together. "What kinds of injuries?"

"Bone fractures. Eleven that he can see. He seems to think it was domestic abuse."

"Domestic abuse?" Her eyes widened, shimmering like beach stones resting just below the surface of the water. "Does that mean I'm married?"

"You weren't wearing a wedding band. But when I found you, you had diapers and baby food in your cart."

"Diapers?" She backed toward the window clinging to the sill. "I have a baby?"

"It's possible," he said, noting that she'd paled several shades. Maybe he shouldn't have said anything. Maybe it was too much all at once.

She shook her head. "No, if I had children I would remember. I couldn't forget something like that."

"You could if you had amnesia."

"You don't understand. I just have this feeling, deep down, that I don't have kids. I can't explain it. It's not that I remember not having kids. But I feel like I would know in my heart if I did, even if I couldn't specifically remember them." She puffed out a long breath, stirring the hair on her forehead. "Does that make *any* sense?"

"It doesn't explain the items in your cart."

"Maybe I was picking them up for someone else. A friend or relative?"

"If that's the case, maybe they'll report you missing."

"Maybe," she said, gnawing her bottom lip with her front teeth. She glanced toward the bathroom door, then back at him. "I, um, need to use the bathroom."

"Okay."

She just stood there, adjusting her weight from one foot to the other.

"Do you want me to leave?" he asked, amused to see her cheeks flush a vibrant pink. He didn't figure her as the type of woman who would embarrass easily. Though she did seem to wear all of her emotions right out on her sleeve.

"Actually, I'm kind of afraid to go in there."

He gestured over his shoulder. "You want me to get a nurse to help you."

"No! I don't need help, I just…this is going to sound *so* lame. I'm afraid of what I'm going to see when I look in the mirror."

"You're afraid you won't recognize yourself?"

"Well, that, too. But I have no idea what I look like."

He frowned. "I'm not following you."

She blew out an exasperated breath. "I could be a *troll*. I could be hideous looking."

He fought the smile tugging at his lips. Just like a woman to worry about beauty. In the looks department, she had *nothing* to worry about. "You're not a troll."

She narrowed her eyes at him. "Oh, yeah? How do I know you're not just saying that to be nice?"

"Because I'm not that nice. Besides, maybe when you look at yourself, you'll remember who you are."

She pressed a hand to her chest, accentuating the swell of two perky breasts under the thin gown. "My heart is pounding like crazy."

Yeah, mine, too, he thought, trying like hell to keep his eyes above her neckline. Which was even worse, because then he had to look at those eyes. Round, innocent and full of uncertainty, they made him want to pull her into his arms and soothe away her fear. It was against his better judgment, and unprofessional, and wrong for about a dozen other reasons he didn't even want to consider, but darn it, he couldn't shake this irrational desire to protect her. He couldn't stop himself from asking, "Want me to go with you?"

With her free arm, she hugged herself. "You think I'm a flake, don't you?"

The truth was, he admired her spirit. She was tough, but not afraid to show her vulnerabilities. And if she was faking her apprehension, she was one hell of an actress. "You've been through a lot. You're holding up better than most people would in your situation." He nodded toward the bathroom, holding out a hand to her. "C'mon. We'll do it together."

She looked at his hand, then over to the bathroom door. "If I pass out, do you promise not to look at my butt? I mean…I don't know what it looks like yet."

It looked okay to me. He caught himself before the words tumbled out of his mouth. He had no right to be talking about her butt. Or looking at it for that matter. She could be someone's wife, someone's mother.

"I promise." He walked to the bathroom and switched on the light. "You'll feel better if you just get it over with."

She shuffled over in bare feet, her face twisting into a grimace as she neared the doorway. He extended his hand, startled by the zing of awareness he experienced when she slipped her cold fingers into his. His first reaction was to yank his hand away, but it was too late to back out now.

Her fingers trembled in his. He tightened his grip, pulling her into the room. "You won't see much with your eyes closed."

"I'm working on it. Just give me a second." She took a long, deep breath, blew it out, and opened her eyes.

She stared at her reflection for the longest time, while Mitch waited for recognition to set in, for a flood of memories to erase the uncertainty so clearly written in her eyes. With her free hand, she reached up and touched her cheek, ran a hand through her disheveled hair.

If he hadn't believed her amnesia story before, it would be tough to refute it now. There was no doubt, she was looking at a total stranger.

"Well?" he asked.

"If it weren't for the fact that you're standing behind me, and I recognize you, I wouldn't know this was me in the mirror. This is so...*weird*." She frowned at her reflection, sticking her tongue out. "At least I'm not a troll. If I had to deal with losing my memory, having an abusive husband, giving birth to children I don't remember *and* being ugly, it would be too much. Oh, and the fact that someone tried to kill me. Can't forget that."

He gave her hand another reassuring squeeze. "We'll figure out who did this."

She looked up at him in the mirror, then down at their clasped hands. "We?"

Poor choice of words. The glimmer of hope in her eyes hit him like a sucker punch. "We as in, the Twin Oaks P.D."

"Ah." She nodded. "Still planning on dumping me somewhere, eh?"

Christ, could she make him feel a little more guilty? He was only doing his job. "I do need to take you to the precinct to get your prints, and I'll take you back to the scene if you feel up to it. Maybe it'll jog your memory."

"Hate to break up the party," someone said from behind them.

They simultaneously jerked their hands free and spun around to see a nurse standing there with a pile of clothes in her arms.

"The doctor signed your release. Try these and see which ones fit. I'll send an orderly in to take you downstairs." She walked over and dropped the clothes on the bed, glancing with unmasked curiosity one last time before she left the room. Mitch was sure he looked guilty as hell. What had possessed him to take Ms. Doe's hand, and even worse, to keep holding it?

Okay, it's not like he didn't have a distant history of this, of letting himself get sucked in emotionally. He had to keep reminding himself, she could be married. Never in a million years would he consciously consider touching another man's wife.

Never *again*. But it hadn't been a conscious decision then, either, had it?

"I'll wait while you get dressed," Mitch said, when the nurse was gone. He walked over to the window, leaving a reasonable distance between them. He looked down at the already crowded parking lot. The rising sun cast a golden glow over the city streets, warming his face through the glass. It would be a beautiful weekend, a weekend he would much rather spend fishing, or working on his yard. And sleeping. God knows he could use a few more hours of uninterrupted sleep.

"Detective?" Ms. Doe said softly.

He turned. She was standing in the bathroom doorway, the clothes stacked in her arms.

"I just wanted to say thanks, you know, for everything. You've been really sweet."

Sweet? He nearly cringed. "I'm only doing my job."

She smiled. She seemed to know as well as he did, he'd gone far above the call of duty.

It wouldn't be the first time.

Mitch watched the video monitor with a deep sense of unease as the man in the hooded jacket stalked Ms. Doe through the store. He carried a basket, taking items from the shelves every so often to appear less suspicious, never getting close enough to be discovered, yet always keeping her in his line of sight. "He keeps his head down, so the camera never gets a shot of his face."

"He knows what he's doing," Marco, the video tech, said.

This was no crime of opportunity. As Mitch had suspected, this had been a cold and calculated attack. But why? "How long does he follow her?"

"About twenty minutes. I spliced the tapes together so we could track their movements." Marco fast-forwarded the tape. "When she leaves the grocery area, he's right behind her. When he's getting ready to strike, he puts the basket down in the middle of the aisle."

"Because he knows we'll eventually be watching

the tape, and if he stashes it on a shelf somewhere we'll find it."

"So why not wear gloves? Then he wouldn't have to worry about leaving prints."

"Why attack her in a well-lit store when he could have done it in a dark parking lot? He's arrogant. He's showing us how cunning he is. He knows that if he puts the stuff in plain sight, some employee will probably see it, pick it up and put the stuff back on the shelves, thus removing any fingerprint evidence."

"And one did. But I'll get to that in a minute. First we have our victim walking down the toy aisle, our suspect is right behind her. Now look, see what he pulls out of his jacket?"

The fluorescent lights glinted off the object in his hand, making its shape clear for several seconds. Mitch mumbled a curse under his breath. "A gun."

He watched as Ms. Doe stopped to pick up a toy. With her back turned, she didn't see the suspect behind her. In a flash of movement, the man coldcocked her in the back of the head, sending her reeling forward. With swift efficiency, he checked her back pockets, then rolled her over to search her jacket. Within seconds, he'd searched her, shoved her small purse in his jacket, and disappeared through a stockroom door.

This was no robbery. He was looking for something specific. And something about the way he searched her disturbed Mitch. Something he couldn't quite put his finger on.

"This isn't good news." He rubbed at a kink in the back of his neck. This was going to be a really long weekend.

"It's about to get worse. Remember your basket theory?" Marco turned to a different monitor, running a second tape. "Here's your basket, sitting there minding its own business, and here's your reliable employee picking it up."

"Tell me she takes it and drops it on a shelf somewhere where we can find it and get prints."

"She drops it all right. Along with any evidence you might have had."

Chapter 4

Mitch watched the monitor as the store employee carried the basket by the toy section, stopped dead in her tracks at the doll aisle, and seconds later dropped the basket on the floor. To the right of the screen he could see his own cart, and himself where he knelt beside Jane Doe.

Aw, *hell*, the basket she'd dropped had belonged to the suspect. Not half an hour later he'd told Greene it wasn't part of the crime scene, which meant someone had probably picked it up and put all the evidence back on the shelves. "Son of a—"

"There's more."

Mitch sunk lower in his chair. "Great."

"He was following her—" Marco paused as he stuck in a different tape "—and she was following you."

Mitch leaned forward, watching himself enter the store, then Ms. Doe only minutes behind him. So it wasn't a coincidence. But what had she wanted from him? What connection could he have to a woman he'd never seen?

"A couple of times she looked like she might approach you, then backed off at the last minute. When you went by the greeting cards, she broke off and went by the toys."

Hell of a detective he was. He hadn't even known he was being followed. He'd been so blasted tired at the time, he could think of nothing but getting home and climbing into bed.

"Kinda weird you ended up on the same aisle as her," Marco said. It wasn't a blatant accusation, but Mitch didn't miss the implication.

"I was looking for a present for Jessica, Darren's little girl. Her fourth birthday party is next weekend."

"Party's been postponed," someone said from behind him. Mitch turned to see Darren Waite, his best friend and fellow detective, leaning casually in the doorway nursing a diet soda. "Heard you caught a case last night."

"She was bashed in the back of the head with a piece by an unknown assailant. And not only can she not ID her attacker, she can't ID herself. She has amnesia."

Darren gestured down the hall. "Was that her in the squad room looking at mugs?"

"Yeah, I'm hoping something might trigger a memory. After I'm finished here, I'm taking her back to the scene."

"I thought this was your weekend off."

"Yeah," he grumbled, "so did I."

"So pass this off to someone else."

"She was following me. She had my name in her pocket. I'm involved somehow and I need to know why."

Darren didn't say anything. He didn't have to. His wary expression said it all.

To circumvent the inevitable lecture he knew was coming, Mitch asked, "So why has the party been postponed?"

"My mother-in-law had a mild heart attack last night. Diane took the girls and flew to Seattle to help out, until she's back on her feet."

"Man, I'm sorry. How long will she be gone?"

"A week or two. Maybe less." Darren downed the last of the soda and tossed the plastic bottle into the trash. "I taped the Tigers game. If you're not busy later, why don't you come by?"

"Honestly, this case is probably going to keep me tied up most of the weekend." Mitch glanced at his watch. It was already close to 11:00 a.m. He had to get back to the store and pick up that stuff for Lisa and his mom, before Lisa had a cow.

"I thought when the rape case broke you were going to take some time off," Darren said.

"I was." Mitch turned to Marco. "Could you print me out a few stills of the suspect?"

"Sure thing." Marco keyed a few commands into the computer and the printer spit out two grainy shots.

Odds were, she wouldn't be able to ID her attacker. But it didn't hurt to maybe show the pictures around, see if anything turned up. The guy could have been anywhere from his early twenties to late forties, was medium height and build, wore grungy clothing. He could be one of ten thousand different men.

"Why don't you pass this case off to Michaels or Petroski?" Darren asked, following Mitch to the squad room. "You haven't had a day off in weeks."

Mitch stopped in the doorway. Ms. Doe was sitting just where he'd left her, a pile of mug books on one side of the desk, a box of doughnuts on the other. The clothes they'd given her at the hospital were acceptable considering they were free, but far from flattering. The shirt was several sizes too big and the threadbare jeans would be down around her ankles if she hadn't taken the tie from her jacket hood and knotted it through the belt loops. Still, there was something about her....

She chose that moment to look up and flash him a thousand-watt smile. After everything she'd been through, she was in surprisingly good spirits. He couldn't deny that he was drawn to her. What man wouldn't be? He also couldn't escape the feeling that she was hiding something.

"She's a doll," Darren said.

Mitch shrugged. "I guess."

"Aw, hell." Darren glanced from Ms. Doe, whose nose was once again buried in the mug book, to Mitch. "You've got a thing for her, don't you?"

"It's not like that."

Darren wasn't buying it. On more than one occasion in the past ten years he'd claimed to know Mitch better than Mitch knew himself. And who knows, maybe he did. They'd gone through the academy together, rode shotgun for two years in uniform, and made detective within a few months of each other. Mitch had been the best man at Darren's wedding, paced anxiously in the waiting room during the birth of his two daughters, Jessica and Lauren, and spent more Sundays than he could remember watching football in the Waites' living room.

In turn, Darren had set him up with just about every one of his wife Diane's single friends. He'd held vigil with him those last few days when Mitch's father had lost his battle with stomach cancer. He was the brother Mitch never had.

"It's not like that," Darren mimicked. "That's what you said before the *Kim* incident."

Mitch did his best not to shudder at the memory. That isolated lapse in judgment would haunt him the rest of his damn life. "This is different. I don't even know who she is. We have reason to believe she's married and has kids. You know I would never get involved with a married woman."

Again. The word hung between them unspoken, but there all the same.

"I'm telling you, don't get yourself mixed up with this one. She's got trouble written all over her. She could be anyone. That guy who attacked her could be her pimp, or her bookie. She could be dealing drugs."

The suspect had seemed anxious to find something. Mitch tried to imagine Ms. Doe pushing drugs, or selling her body on a street corner. She looked more like a kindergarten teacher than a criminal.

"She could be faking the amnesia," Darren said. "Jerking you around."

"Yeah, I considered that. Every now and then she'll say something and, I don't know, it makes me wonder if she's not just making it up. But then there are times when she seems genuinely scared and confused. You should have seen her expression when she looked in the mirror. Not to mention that she puked on me when she realized she didn't know her own name."

In his pocket, his pager vibrated. He pulled it out and looked at the display. "It's Lisa. She's already paged me five times this morning. She probably left fifty messages on my voice mail."

"How's your mom doing? She and Lisa kill each other yet?"

"Not yet. Of course, I haven't talked to her today."

"Well, I'm outta here. I figure I'll get some stuff done around the house while Diane is gone." He laid a hand on Mitch's shoulder. "Watch yourself with Jane Doe. I have a bad feeling about this one."

So did Mitch. But not bad enough to scare him off the case. He needed to know what possible connection they could have to each other. "As soon as we revisit the crime scene, I'm going to get her settled in a halfway house."

"Using the one on Lexington?" Darren asked, and Mitch nodded. "That place isn't so bad. Besides, someone will probably report her missing when she doesn't show up for work Monday, right?"

"That's what I'm hoping." But deep down, something told him he wouldn't be getting off that easily.

Undetected, he watched as she thumbed through the pages of the mug book. She was wasting her time. She wouldn't find him in there. He was a master of the game, beyond detection or retribution. Minutes ago, she'd looked right at him, made eye contact even, and there wasn't the slightest reaction.

After leaving the store, he'd searched her house for hours last night, tearing through one room after another. He'd found nothing to tell him where she kept them. She was smart for a woman.

But not smart enough.

He did find something else. Something that might come in handy later when his possessions were safely returned. He'd found the perfect way to put her in her place, to show her who was in charge.

The perfect conclusion to the game.

Jane glanced over at Detective Thompson. He'd changed into jeans and a flannel shirt, and though the denim hugged his long, lean legs and the shirt accentuated those strong, sturdy shoulders, she would miss the hospital scrubs.

He stood by the door, deep in conversation with the Arnold Palmer wanna-be. Though Arnold looked like he should be out on the fairway chasing golf balls, the ease and authority with which he carried himself in the station told her that he was another cop. They spoke quietly to one another, looking over at her every so often.

For police detectives they weren't terribly subtle in their exchange. She would have to be a complete moron not to realize she was the topic of conversation. Or maybe they just didn't care if she knew. Maybe it was some kind of "good cop/bad cop" routine.

She watched as Detective Thompson yawned and scratched his unshaven chin. He couldn't have gotten much sleep last night, and like her, he looked as if he could use a long hot shower.

Hmm. Now, there was an interesting visual: Detective Thompson in the shower…

Shame on you, she scolded herself. You could be married. Yeah, to a wife-beater. Wouldn't that be great. She just couldn't believe she would let a man push her around that way. She had to believe that if what the doctors said was true and she'd suffered domestic abuse, she'd left the jerk a long time ago. If not, what reason did she have to get her memory back? What kind of life would she have to go back to?

Her children—if they really existed. That was another thing that just didn't feel right to her. What mother could forget her kids?

Her stomach rumbled, and she looked over at the box of doughnuts Detective Thompson had set there. They just weren't cutting it. Maybe she could talk him into springing for lunch before he dumped her. Until she figured out who she was, she was at the mercy of the Twin Oaks Police department. Having no money, no clothing that fit right—*no identity*—drove her nuts with frustration.

She felt Detective Thompson's presence beside her before he made a sound. The air crackled with energy whenever he was near, raising the hair on her arms. She looked up and was instantly caught in his liquid brown eyes. She sizzled like fire from the tips of her toes to the roots of her hair and everywhere in between.

He was definitely the good cop in this scenario.

"Any luck?" he asked, pulling up a chair. He spun it around and straddled the seat, resting his arms on the back. He'd rolled his sleeves to the elbows, exposing muscular, sun-bronzed forearms. His hands were large, his fingers long and graceful-looking. She could just imagine what those hands could do to a woman. What they could do to *her*.

Swallowing hard, she closed the book. "Sorry, nothing."

"Think you're ready to go back to the scene?"

Her stomach contracted with a sudden stab of fear. "I—I think so."

"If you're scared, or you're just not ready, we don't have to go today."

Did he have to be so understanding, so…sweet? If he forced her, if he made her go, she wouldn't have a choice. She would have to face her fear.

She took a deep, fortifying breath. Forced or not, she needed to do this. The answers were locked away somewhere in her traumatized brain. Maybe that store would be the key.

"I want to go," she said, infusing her voice with confidence. "Does this little excursion possibly include lunch? If I have to face my demons, I probably shouldn't do it on an empty stomach."

He gestured to the box beside her. "What, you don't like doughnuts?"

"I'm sure it's a staple item for you, but I need something a little more substantial. Preferably something that mooed in a former life."

He flashed her an easy grin. He didn't smile often, but when he did...*wow*. "I guess it's safe to assume you're not a vegetarian."

"I'm thinking that I'm probably not."

"Any place in particular you'd like to go?"

Good question. Did she have a favorite restaurant? Did she prefer fast food? Fine dining? Ethnic or American?

She gave it some thought, her mind colliding with that infuriating brick wall. She shrugged, hating the words even before they left her mouth. "I guess I'll have to trust your judgment."

Mitch watched with fascination as Ms. Doe popped the last bite of the double cheeseburger in her mouth. For someone so petite, she sure could put away the food.

She gestured to his French fries. "You planning to finish those?"

He slid his plate across the table.

She squeezed out a glob of ketchup and dipped one in. "So what if I get to the store and don't remember anything? What's our next move?" She noticed his wary look and corrected herself. "I mean *your* next move. Can't you run my picture on the news or in the paper? Maybe someone will recognize me."

"Not a good idea. Not until we figure who's behind this. They could use the amnesia to get to you."

"Oh. I didn't think of that."

"It hasn't even been twenty-four hours. Any official missing-person report wouldn't be filed for at least forty-eight. Don't give up hope. We could have you back with your family soon."

She frowned, shaking her head lightly.

"What's wrong?"

"It's this whole family thing. It just doesn't feel right. I keep thinking I would know if I had children."

"I guess we'll just have to wait and see."

"Stretch marks," she said, pointing a ketchup-soaked fry in his direction. "If I had children, wouldn't I have stretch marks? Because I checked every inch of my body when I was getting dressed and I couldn't find any. My skin is practically flawless."

Every inch, huh? And all of it flawless. He'd been doing his best not to think about her in those terms, or imagine seeing all of that flawless skin firsthand—the parts he hadn't already seen, that is. And here she had to go and bring it up, putting all sorts of improper thoughts into his head.

"I know that probably sounds arrogant," she added, "but it is very nice skin."

He nodded. "Hmm."

"I have a nice butt, too," she said, popping the fry in her mouth. "Not spectacular, mind you, but I don't feel so bad about you seeing it back in the hospital."

He nearly choked on his coffee. "I didn't—"

"Of course you did. My gown was hanging open, and you were standing behind me. How could you *not* look? If our roles had been reversed and it was your butt hanging out *I* would have looked."

He leaned back in the booth. "Is that so?"

"Back at the station, when they were fingerprinting me, you bent over to pick up something and I looked at your butt then."

He stifled a grin. The woman was shameless. It was one of the things he liked most about her. And the thing that was probably going to get him into trouble. "Did you?"

"It's human nature to look." She waved a hand in the air. "Hormones or pheromones or something." She paused, her brow furrowing. "What was my point?"

"Stretch marks?"

"Exactly. So if I had ever been pregnant, I would have at least a few stretch marks. Therefore we can safely deduce that I don't have children."

"What about adoption?"

She popped the last fry in her mouth looking thoughtful. "Darn, I never thought of that. You know, you're pretty good at this detective stuff."

"That's what they tell me." He took a long swallow of coffee then signaled the waitress for the check. His pager began to tremble and he pulled it from his pocket, cursing when he read the display. "We'd better get going."

"Pressing business?"

He tossed change on the table for a tip. "You could say that."

He paid the bill and she followed him out to the unmarked, run-of-the-mill blue sedan they'd driven over from the station. As badly as she wanted this to be over, as much as she wanted her life back, the possibilities frightened her. Suppose she was married to a wife-beater, or someone even worse. Something too horrible to put into words.

"You okay?" Detective Thompson was holding the door, waiting for her to get in.

She plastered a smile on her face. "Fine."

She could tell he didn't believe her. He touched her shoulder, giving it a gentle squeeze. Though she was sure the gesture was meant only to comfort, the weight of his hand made the skin beneath tingle.

"We won't do more than what you're ready for," he said.

Could the guy be any nicer? He waited until she was in, then closed the door.

"I don't suppose I could talk you into loaning me the money for some new clothes," she said when he climbed in the driver's side. "I'm good for it…I think."

"Buckle up." He waited until she fastened her seat belt then started the car and pulled out of the lot. "What's wrong with the clothes you have on?"

"You're joking, right?"

A grin flirted at the corner of his mouth. "I'm sure they'll have something more suitable for you at the half-way house."

They drove along in silence for a minute, then Mitch reached into his jacket pocket and pulled out a sheet of paper. "I'd like you to look at something. It's a still shot from the security tape."

Tentatively, she took the photo. "So this is the man who attacked me?"

"I know the picture quality is poor, but does he look familiar?"

"No. Not at all." She felt relieved and disappointed all at once. She handed the picture back. "Sorry."

He folded it up and shoved it into his pocket. "It was worth a shot."

He made a sharp right into a parking lot, and when she looked at the Save Mart sign looming above, her heart began to pound wildly in her chest. She gasped, clutching the edge of the seat.

"Something wrong?" he asked.

As quickly as the sensation had gripped her, it disappeared. "I don't know. For a second there, I thought my heart was going to jump out of my chest. I think I may have remembered something."

He pulled into a spot close to the door, threw the car into Park and turned to her. "Does the store look familiar?"

She peered out the side window at the aging brick building. "Yes and no. When I look at it, I instinctively know what kind of store it is, but I can't say that I've ever been here."

"So it *does* look familiar?"

"Sort of, but…" She paused, searching for the words to explain. It was difficult to describe something she barely understood. "If you took me to a gas station I'd never been to before, I would still know it was a gas station. This store is familiar, but only in the sense that I know what type of store it is."

"Do you want to try going inside?"

"We're here. I may as well give it a shot."

She waited for him to walk around and open her door, delaying the inevitable for a few precious seconds. Not only was she afraid of what she may or may not discover about her past, but her time with Detective Thompson had nearly expired. If she didn't get her memory back now, he would dump her at some halfway house. Then she would really be alone.

She swallowed back the fear crawling up from her belly.

Her door swung open and, steeling herself for what was to come—good or bad—she climbed out. The sun had disappeared behind a line of ominous dark clouds and a chilling dampness skittered the length of her spine. Was it some divine warning? Did she even believe in God? Was she Catholic, Jewish, Muslim?

So many questions and still no answers.

"You sure you're okay with this?" Detective Thompson asked once again.

"I'm sure," she said, feeling anything but. Feeling instead as if she'd like to run in the opposite direction, back to the car. Or better yet, into Detective Thompson's arms. She was reasonably sure she would feel safe there. However, if she planned to get through this ordeal in one piece, she could rely on only one person.

Herself. Wasn't that the way it had always been?

She stopped dead in her tracks, struggling to hold on to the thought, but it was already slipping away. That had been a memory, she was sure of it. But what did it mean?

A car horn blared and a hand wrapped around her upper arm, yanking her out of the way. "Earth to Jane."

She looked up into Detective Thompson's concerned face. Only then did she realize she'd stopped right in the middle of the lot, blocking traffic.

"What's wrong?" he asked.

"I don't know. I…I think I remembered something. But it was more like a feeling than an actual memory."

"What did it feel like."

"I felt…*alone*."

"You're not alone."

"Not yet."

If she saw a flash of guilt in his eyes, it was gone almost instantly. "Let's go inside."

They stepped through the automatic door and she once again felt that sudden and brief surge of adrenaline.

"I think I remember being here," she said, excitement and hope erupting inside of her like a geyser. Maybe it would all start to come back now. Maybe this nightmare was almost over.

Or maybe it was just beginning.

Chapter 5

"Is it familiar?" Detective Thompson asked.

"I think so. I don't even know how I know it," Jane said. "I just…feel it."

"We'll try retracing your path through the store. While we're here, I'm going to pick up a few things." He grabbed a cart and pointed it in the direction of the grocery department, swerving to avoid a pack of unruly teenagers and a shell-shocked mother with three rowdy children. Being a Saturday afternoon, the store was loud and bustling with activity.

They started in the produce section where he extracted a crumpled list from his jacket pocket. She walked alongside him while he shopped, taking in her surroundings, willing herself to remember. It felt so close, like she could brush it with her fingertips, yet too far to get a grasp on. Every time she reached further, strained to touch it, it slipped further away from her. She was thinking so forcefully her head began to throb.

He seemed to pick up on her distress. "Relax. Try to let it come naturally."

She felt like screaming and stamping her feet. She didn't want to relax. She wanted this to be over with. She wanted to remember *now*. "I wish I could put into words how frustrating this is. It's like hearing a melody in your head, and knowing there are words to go along with it, but you just can't remember what they are."

"When that happens to me, I try to think about something else, and usually the words come to me when I least expect it."

There was a definite logic to that. Maybe she was trying *too* hard. She'd thought of nothing else since waking in the hospital that morning.

"So tell me about yourself, Detective." At his curious glance, she added, "If we talk about you for a while, maybe I'll stop thinking about me. Right?"

"Okay." He tossed a bag of baby carrots in the cart. "What do you want to know?"

"What do you want to tell me?"

He shrugged. "Not much to tell, really. I'm not married. I live alone. I love my job. That's about it."

"Do you have family?"

"My mom and my sister." He consulted the list and headed for a bin of broccoli.

"Are you close to them?"

"Since my dad died I've kind of taken over as the head of the family. When my mom had back surgery a few weeks ago, Lisa moved in with her. I do most of the running around."

"That must put a damper on your social life."

He barked out a rueful laugh. "What social life?"

"That doesn't bother your girlfriend?"

"Might if I had one."

No girlfriend? How could a man as sweet and attractive as Detective Thompson *not* have one? Unless girls weren't his thing.

Jane gave him a sideways glance, watched him walk—the casual, sturdy swagger. She would bet her last dollar he was one hundred percent heterosexual male. The other obvious explanation would be a prior failed relationship.

"Ever been married?" she asked.

There was a slight pause before he said, "Almost."

His total blank expression made her realize how hard he was trying not to look wounded.

Way to go, Jane. Any other painful past experiences you'd like to dredge up? Maybe a favorite family pet he'd had to euthanize? "I'm sorry, that was insensitive of me."

"It's okay, it was a long time ago. I'm married to my work now."

"Sounds lonely."

They fell silent. She walked beside him, watching in her peripheral vision as he dropped items in his cart. It didn't escape her attention the appraising looks he attracted from women. Appraising being a major understatement. Jaws dropped and tongues lolled. Not that she didn't relate. He was ridiculously easy on the eyes.

The unshaven chin, slightly mussed hair and faded

blue jeans gave him a roguish edge, like that irresistible bad boy mothers forbade their daughters to date, yet everything else about him screamed dependable and safe. It was probably the intense yet patient way he looked at a person, until they felt compelled to confess their most horrific sins.

Married to his work? It was a damn shame to waste all of that raw sex appeal.

"You're awfully quiet," he said. "Thinking about your past?"

"Actually, no. I was thinking about sex appeal."

One eyebrow lifted. "Dare I ask whose?"

"Yours."

"I have sex appeal?"

She rolled her eyes. "You can't tell me you don't notice the way women look at you. On a scale of one to ten, you're about an eleven on the studmuffin-ometer."

"Studmuffin-ometer?" He narrowed his eyes at her. "Is this like the butt thing?"

"I'll bet you had a lot of girlfriends in high school."

He turned down the laundry aisle, choosing a box of powdered detergent and a bottle of fabric softener. "Why is that?"

"You look trustworthy. Women like a guy who makes them feel safe."

She had his undivided attention now. He stopped walking and turned to her. *"I'm* safe?"

She propped her hands on her hips, giving him a thorough once-over. "I think it's the big, brown puppy-dog eyes. And you have good manners. I'll bet you always ask permission before you kiss a woman."

He shook his head. "Are you always this brutally honest?"

"I don't know. Does it bother you?"

"No." He started down the aisle. "Truthfully, it's refreshing for a change. Women usually play games."

"Sounds like you've been hanging around with the wrong women."

"Yeah, it's a gift. I'm like a magnet."

"Besides, what do I have to gain by playing games? I figure, if I'm totally honest with you, maybe you'll show me the same courtesy."

"You want total honesty?"

Something in his tone made the hair raise on her arms. "When you say it like that, I don't know."

He leaned down, until she felt his breath shift the hair next to her ear. "In the hospital, I did look." With a wolfish grin he glanced meaningfully at her backside. "And you were wrong. It is spectacular."

Oh, my. She'd never imagined him looking so…predatory. This was definitely a side of him she hadn't expected.

"Ooookay," she conceded, a flush warming her cheeks, "maybe you're not quite as safe as I assumed."

"No, I'm human. And human nature," he said, "can be a damn fine thing."

He stopped again, and she realized they were standing in front of the feminine products. He gazed up at the shelves, looking perplexed.

She peeked over at his list. "Ultra-absorbent, huh?"

"They're not for me."

She laughed. "Gosh, I hope not."

"This is my sister's list." He looked at the list, then over at the shelf, shifting uncomfortably.

She selected a box and tossed it in the cart for him. "If I had a brother and he'd done something unspeakable to me, like you've obviously done to her, I would make him buy my tampons, too."

He flattened a hand over his chest. "Who, me? The safe guy? The—hey, wait a minute, you just said *if* you had a brother. Does that mean you don't?"

She clutched the side of the cart. "I don't know. Maybe I don't." That familiar burst of hope rushed to the surface, and just as swiftly fizzled away behind a cloud of uncertainty. If she did or didn't have a brother—or a surgically removed Siamese twin for that matter—it was a mystery to her. How could she expect to remember siblings when she couldn't remember her own children?

Tears of frustration stung her eyes. "I hate this."

"Why don't we try the aisle where I found you? Are you ready for that?"

She nodded and wiped her face with the sleeve of her jacket. "I just want this to be over with."

"According to the security cameras you went this way," he said, leading her past the cosmetic department and through housewares. "You stopped to look at cooking utensils, but never put anything in your cart. Then you headed to the toys."

She followed him through the toy department, waiting for recognition to set in, for a surge of memories to resurface. If nothing else, the blank space seemed to expand, swallowing up any sense of familiarity she'd felt before.

Mitch stopped at the end of the doll aisle, looking back at her. "You don't remember."

"Nothing so far. Where did you find me?"

"This *is* where I found you," he said, pointing to the floor. "Right there."

"Oh," she said softly, defeat clear in her tone. She looked so lost standing there, Mitch had to fight the urge to pull her into his arms and comfort her. She'd had such hope, but the secrets locked in her subconscious must have been buried deep.

"Hey, don't worry. It'll come back to you." He tried to keep his voice reassuring, but he couldn't deny his own disappointment. If her memory had returned he would be taking her home. Now he had no choice but to drop her off at the halfway house, where nothing was likely to jar her memory. He was doing his job, yet he couldn't dodge a knife of guilt. Maybe Darren had been right. Maybe he should have pawned this off on someone else. He was already too involved.

"Can we go now?" she asked, folding her arms around herself.

"Sure. Let's go."

She walked beside him to the registers, head bowed. "I'm sorry I've wasted all this time."

"You didn't waste anything. Investigating a crime means checking out every possible angle or lead. That can mean hitting a lot of dead ends. Eventually something will pan out."

"I wish I shared your confidence."

"You have to trust me," he said.

"I don't want to put that kind of trust in anyone.

Right now, I don't even trust myself." A tear slipped down her cheek and she brushed it away. "Darn it. I don't want to do this here."

As they rounded the corner, he saw that every open checkout lane was lined three to four carts deep. It would take an eternity to get through. Jane stood behind him, her jaw clenched. She was teetering on the edge of an emotional meltdown, yet she didn't implore him to leave or utter a word of complaint.

Christ, how did he get himself into this mess? He had two choices—neither of which he was all that thrilled about. He could make Jane tough it out and hope like hell she could hold it together. Or, he could get her out of there and risk Lisa's wrath. God only knew what she'd make him buy next time. Either way, it boiled down to what he was more afraid of. An overwrought, overly emotional amnesiac on the verge of tears, or his sister.

He shoved the cart behind a rack of women's clothing and cupped a hand under Jane's elbow, leading her toward the door.

She stumbled, surprised by their sudden speed. "Wh-where are we going?"

"I'm getting you out of here."

"But—" she glanced back over her shoulder "—what about your groceries?"

He guided her through the door and out into the parking lot. "I'll come back later."

Inky clouds hung threateningly low and thunder rumbled in the distance. The pavement was damp, the air chilled and heavy with the scent of rain. He walked her to the car and helped her inside.

"That was very sweet of you," she said when he got in.

There it was again, that annoying word. "I am *not* sweet." He started the car, switched on the wipers and cranked the heat up full blast. "Think like a man for a minute. If you were in a crowded store with a woman who was about to burst into tears, what would you have done?"

"Gotten the hell out as fast as I could?"

"Exactly."

"In other words, your actions were purely selfish."

When he looked over at her, she was grinning. "You don't believe me?"

"I believe that you'd like to believe that. I also believe that you were being sweet. You're a nice guy, Detective. Why can't you just admit it?"

Mitch clutched the steering wheel, his jaw tense. "If you knew me, you'd feel differently."

Any minute now.

Jane listened to the bed creak and groan as she shifted her weight, attempting in vain to avoid the springs jabbing her in the back. There was something about this place. Something disturbingly familiar, like the ghost of a long past memory. It wasn't even the room itself she seemed to recognize, but the atmosphere. The essence of stale cigarette smoke and mold. The impersonal ambience that made a place feel cold and temporary.

She gazed up at the maze of cracks and craters that barely passed for a ceiling, guessing that it might have been white at one time, and praying it didn't choose that particular moment for its inevitable collapse. What paint hadn't peeled off had faded to a dingy, dirty gray and water damage warped three of the four corners. The fourth corner had dark splatter stains that might have been...well, she didn't really want to know what they were. Just like she wouldn't venture to guess the origin of similar stains she'd found on the sheets when she'd dared pull back the threadbare comforter.

Apparently the nicer halfway house—talk about an oxymoron—had no available space. Mitch had apologized for the dreary conditions, explaining that the city had limited funds and not enough crime to warrant building a new facility. Luxurious it wasn't, but for the time being she was trapped here.

Very soon, that would change.

The director of the halfway house—a female physical equivalent of a sumo wrestler—had assured Detective Thompson she wouldn't let Jane out of the house. Though getting past the woman might prove to be a challenge, outrunning her would be a piece of cake. Unfortunately, Jane didn't want the police alerted to her self-imposed liberation. Her only hope was a stealthy escape.

They were bound to discover her absence eventually. Hopefully by then she'd be long gone. Her room was on the first floor and the window opened to the back alley. She would simply slide it open and hop down. She couldn't see the harm in taking a walk around town, maybe give her memory a much needed nudge. If her attacker had no clue as to her whereabouts, as Detective Thompson had assured her, how could he possibly know where to look for her? She would be perfectly safe.

She rolled out of bed and pushed back the tattered,

sun-faded curtains. The storm had blown over, leaving dreary skies and a bone-chilling dampness in its wake. She'd wait a few more minutes to be sure Detective Thompson was long gone. Checking the pocket of her jacket, she found the business card he'd given her.

"In case you need anything," he'd said when he handed it to her.

Need anything? Ha! What she *needed* was to find out who she was. Still, it would be good to keep his number handy. If she ran into any trouble or, God forbid, got lost, she'd find a pay phone and call him collect—save him the trouble of looking for her later.

She glanced at the glowing red numbers on the digital clock next to the bed. He'd been gone twenty minutes. That should give her a pretty good head start. Dressed in the clothes the halfway house director had given her—clothes that actually fit—and with the hood of her jacket up, there was a good chance she could go unrecognized.

She rolled out of bed, locked the door to her room, then unfastened the latch on the window. With some effort she pried it up far enough to stick her head out. As far as she could see in either direction the alley was deserted. So far so good. But boy was it a *long* way down—six feet at least with nothing but asphalt to cushion her landing. One wrong move and she could bust an ankle or twist a knee.

Come on Jane, don't be a chicken.

She'd come too far to back out now. Putting all her weight behind the effort, she pushed open the window. She stuck one foot out, then the other, until she was sitting, both legs dangling out the window. It was now or never.

One…two… she closed her eyes and shoved…*three!*

She hit the slippery asphalt at a slight angle. Both feet flew out from under her and she went down hard on her behind. Not exactly graceful in her execution, but nothing appeared to be broken. And better still, she was *free*.

Or was she?

She sensed a presence before she saw him emerge from the side of the building.

"Going somewhere?"

Chapter 6

"You scared me half to death!"

Jane looked cute sitting on the ground under the window, glaring up at him. Pissed off, but cute. And right now, Mitch wanted to tan her hide. He should have known she wasn't going to make this easy for him.

He did know.

Mitch extended a hand to her. "Need a boost?"

He grabbed her hand, ignoring the softness of her skin, and the distinct urge to pull her straight into his arms and hold her—an urge he seemed to be feeling a lot lately—and hiked her to her feet.

"I thought you left," she said, brushing dirt and gravel from the seat of her jeans.

"That's what you were supposed to think. Call it intuition, but I had a feeling you might try something."

"I watched you drive away."

"I parked around the block and walked back."

She looked up at the window then back at him. "I don't suppose you'd believe it if I said I accidentally fell out."

"Don't suppose I would." He leaned against the building, folding his arms across his chest. "That was a stupid move. Short of posting an armed guard outside your window, I don't suppose there was any chance of you staying put."

She imitated his stance, adding a stubborn lift of her chin. "I'm thinking, no, probably not."

She was going to mess around and get herself hurt. "I can't stand guard under your window *and* investigate your case."

"Then let me go. Pretend you never saw me jump out the window. It'll be our little secret."

"I can't do that."

She let out a long, exaggerated sigh. "Then we've got a dilemma, because wherever you take me, I'm going to find a way to escape."

Any amusement he'd been feeling was instantly replaced with an inexplicable urge to shake some sense into her. Her habit of constantly second-guessing him irritated and intrigued him all at once. "That would be a *really* bad idea."

"So you keep telling me. But I'm not going to sit around doing nothing. It's not like I'm under arrest. You can't force me."

"There's been a new development."

"Oh, yeah—what?"

"Someone claiming to be me called the hospital and was asking questions about you. About the amnesia."

Her voice lost that just-try-and-mess-with-me edge. "You think it was the man who did this to me?"

"Whoever it was knew which hospital to call, he knew to use my name and he had information that could have only been obtained in the case file. There was something about the security tape that was bugging me. I finally figured out what it was. When the suspect searched you, he patted you down."

She shrugged. "I don't get it."

"He looked like a cop, Jane. Either he was a cop, or still is. If that's the case, he may have contacts in the precinct. Hell, he could work there for all I know, which could mean that he knows where we're hiding you."

Now he had her attention. She glanced nervously up and down the length of the alley. "You don't really think he'll come after me…do you?"

"He was looking for something when he attacked you. I don't think he found it."

She tugged at her bottom lip with her teeth. "So I am in danger."

Her teeth left white impressions in her rosy lip. He imagined what it would be like to nibble on those lips, like the forbidden fruit that they were. Curious as he might have been, it was out of the question, for his sake as much as hers.

"Until we figure out who did this to you and why, you're not really safe here at this halfway house, either." He didn't want to alarm her. God knows she had enough to worry about already, but he couldn't risk her taking off on him again. His instincts were telling him she'd gotten herself mixed up in something or with someone with ties to the police. Meaning, from here on in, he didn't know who he could trust.

And until she remembered something, finding out who did this was going to be a painful process of elimination.

She tipped her head and looked up at him through narrowed eyes. "Until *we* figure it out? You mean you and the Twin Oaks police?"

"The truth is, I'm at a dead end. We need to work on getting your memory back. We, as in you and me."

A smug smile curled the corners of her mouth. "In other words, you need me."

"Yeah," he conceded. "I need you." Surprisingly, the words weren't nearly as hard to say as he'd expected. He didn't want to *need* anyone. Especially someone like her. One wrong move and he could kiss his badge goodbye.

"I could say I told you so, but I won't."

He grinned and nodded to the open window. "Anything you need to go back for?"

She shot the window a scathing look. "Nothing I can't live without."

"We should go." He didn't like the idea of hanging out in an alley, even in broad daylight. He never knew who might be watching.

"Not to another halfway house?"

"I'm yours for the day. Tonight you'll stay in a safe house. Fair enough?"

"Fair enough."

They started walking, but she stopped suddenly, a puzzled look on her face.

"What's wrong?" Mitch asked.

"If I wasn't safe here, why didn't you come inside and get me? Why did you wait until I climbed out the window."

"Like I said, I had the feeling you were up to something. I thought it might be fun to wait and see what you planned to do. I was going to give you five more minutes, then come in."

For a minute she looked like she might belt him, then a reluctant smile crept across her face. "I guess I deserved that. What tipped you off, by the way?"

"You were so against coming here, I figured I'd have to drag you in kicking and screaming. When you didn't so much as bat an eyelash, I knew you had something planned. Sneaking away seemed the logical next move, and somehow I couldn't see you strolling out the front door."

"And you were right."

"Yeah, well, that happens every now and then." He started walking again and she fell in step beside him. "I get the distinct impression that when you want something, you don't let anyone or anything get in your way."

"Is that a good or a bad thing?"

"I guess that all depends on what you want."

"Oh, I know what I want. The question is, what do *you* want, Detective?"

He looked down at her and for a moment their eyes locked. Hers were soft and intelligent and wise beyond their years. Did she know just by looking at him? Could she tell he knew exactly what he wanted, even though he also knew he could never have it? It was all the more reason to keep his priorities clear.

He forced himself to look away. "I want to solve your case. That's it."

He was lying. Jane could see it in his eyes. This attraction she'd been feeling was no longer one-sided. Maybe it never had been. But she was pretty sure he wasn't the type of cop to fraternize with a victim of a crime he was investigating. He was way too by-the-book for that.

Beside her, Mitch swore. He grabbed her roughly and threw her against the side of the Dumpster they were walking past, knocking the breath from her lungs. Covering her body with his own, he pinned her there. She cried out as the unforgiving metal cut into her back.

Fear, paralyzing and absolute, clutched at her gut, twisting it inside out. For a second she was too bewildered to react. With him plastered against her, she could barely breathe. All she could think was, *not again. Please not again.* Instinct kicked in and adrenaline rushed through her veins. She shoved hard against his chest and screamed. "Let me go!"

"Shhh!" he hissed, clasping a hand over her mouth. She sunk her teeth into his palm, tasting the salty tang of his skin. He grunted but didn't let go. Then she noticed the barrel of his gun not three inches from her face and her jaw went slack. It wasn't pointed at her, but that didn't make it look any less intimidating.

"Are you going to yell again?" he whispered.

She shook her head and he dropped his hand. She tasted blood, meaning she'd definitely broken the skin. Oh boy, he looked mad, too.

"Keep quiet and don't move," he whispered gruffly. He edged his way to the corner of the Dumpster, his weapon drawn and poised in front of him. He'd barely cleared the side when she heard a loud ping. Then another, closer. He darted back, resuming his original position, cursing under his breath.

That's when it began to sink in—the pings she'd heard were bullets hitting the Dumpster. Someone was *shooting* at them!

His body resting protectively around her, Detective Thompson pulled out his phone and quickly dialed 911.

Jane clutched the lapels of his jacket, shaking from the inside out, heart beating wildly. Here she'd thought he was attacking her, when in reality he was trying to protect her. He shielded her body in a way that, if any bullets flew in their direction, they would hit him, not her. And she'd given him a flesh wound for his trouble.

The next few minutes seemed to go on forever, until she heard the faint wail of a police siren approaching. The frantic beating of her heart began to cease as the sound got louder, as their salvation came closer.

Against her, she felt Detective Thompson heave a sigh of relief, then back away. She was so frozen with fear, he had to pry her hands from his jacket.

"I think he's gone. You okay?"

She nodded, her head feeling loose and wobbly on her neck.

Through gritted teeth, he asked, "Next time I tell you to do something, think maybe you could do it?"

She nodded again.

"And the next time you feel like sinking your teeth into someone, try to remember, I'm one of the *good* guys."

"I'm so sorry," she said, her voice trembling. "I don't know what came over me. I...I panicked."

She reached for his hand, but he jerked it away.

"I'm fine."

"Let me look." After a bit of grumbling on his part, he relinquished his hand to her. There was an awful lot of blood. She wiped the wound clean with the sleeve of her jacket.

He sucked in a breath and yanked his hand away, shaking off the pain as the first squad car came to a screeching halt at the end of the alley. "I'm fine."

Within seconds two more cars joined the first and she had the surreal impression she'd just walked on the set of a movie. This couldn't really be happening to her. Someone couldn't be trying to shoot her.

What had she gotten herself into?

Mitch signaled the officers with some complicated hand motion and gestured in the direction the shots had come from.

"You saved my life," she said, feeling a weak-kneed brand of relief that made it difficult to hold herself upright.

"No, if he wanted to kill you, he would have. He's messing with your head."

And doing a fair job of it. "How did you even know he was there?"

"When the first bullet hit the ground next to my foot."

How could he stand there so calmly, like he was talking about the weather? "By your foot? I didn't hear a shot. Come to think of it, I didn't hear *any* shots."

He leaned on the Dumpster beside her, gun still drawn and resting by his side. "He used a silencer."

A uniformed officer appeared at the corner of the Dumpster. "No sign of him, Detective. No shells, no witnesses."

"Of course not." He holstered his weapon. "Canvas the area and page me if you find something."

"Officer Martin will give you a ride back to the precinct."

"I can take my own car back."

"Not with four slashed tires, you can't."

He looked calm on the outside, but Jane could see a storm brewing behind his eyes as he turned to her and hooked a hand around her arm. "Let's go."

She nearly had to jog to keep up with him as he led her to one of the squad cars. "Where are we going?"

"To the precinct. I'll have to file a report and get a new vehicle."

"Then where?"

"Somewhere he can't find us."

"Detective, how are you going to find him if you're baby-sitting me?"

He wrenched the car door open. "My main priority right now is keeping you safe."

Safe? She couldn't imagine the concept. She hadn't felt safe since she woke up in the middle of this mess. "And how do you plan on doing that?"

He turned to her, his eyes dark and foreboding. "Very carefully."

* * *

Did they really think they could hide her?

Fools.

They were wasting their time searching for him. He'd been long gone before the first car reached the scene. He was untouchable.

It made him sick, the way they doted on her, felt sorry for her. Bitch. *If they only knew, they wouldn't be trying to protect her. They would put her in a cell. Lock her away. Tonight he would make his move. And there would be no one to stop him.*

"So you really don't remember *anything?*" Mitch's sister, Lisa, set a cup of coffee in front of Jane and slid into a chair on the opposite side of the small dining table.

"Give her a break, Lisa," Mitch warned. He stood in the kitchen, cleaning the bite wound on his hand under his mother's kitchen faucet.

"I don't mind," Jane said, her hands still trembling slightly as she gripped the cup. "No, I don't remember a thing. Just vague impressions every now and then."

Lisa leaned back in her chair, tossing a mane of bleach-blond hair over her shoulder. Her T-shirt stretched tight across her generous bust and proclaimed in bold type The Dark Is Afraid Of Me. "Wow, I can't imagine forgetting my own name. That must really suck."

"You have no idea." Jane lifted the cup and sniffed, scrunching her nose. She instinctively knew she wouldn't like it. She was finding a lot of things to be second nature. Like driving—although not the back seat kind Detective Thompson had accused her of. Though she hadn't actually gotten behind the wheel yet, she knew what to do.

And she knew Detective Thompson, despite having met less than a day ago. There was a familiarity there that she felt deep inside her bones—some strange cosmic connection linking them to one another. Not that she necessarily believed in mystical cosmic forces. Or maybe she did, who knows? She only knew that when they were together, the air around them felt electrically charged.

There was no question he felt it, too, and he'd made it clear, in his own subtle way, that he was off-limits. And who could blame him for his caution? What reason did he have to trust her? She didn't even know if she could trust herself.

Shelving the urge to indulge in another bout of self-pity, she gazed around the kitchen and the cozy family room beyond. If the pictures that lined the expanse of one wall were any indication, not much had changed in the past twenty or so years. She could easily imagine the detective as a teenager, slouched into one of the two plaid couches in the living room, watching television— a bag of chips on one side, the remote on the other.

Jane had to wonder if she'd grown up in a house like this. Had she been rich, poor, middle-class? Had the air been tinged with the scent of potpourri and furniture polish? Had she lounged on a plaid couch watching television or doing her homework? The need for answers was so intense it burned like wildfire deep in her soul and filled her with a fidgety frustration.

There was *one* thing she did know for sure, Jane realized, putting her cup down. She didn't like coffee.

"Too strong?" Lisa asked.

She pushed it away. "I don't think I'm a coffee drinker. Sorry."

"How long has Mom been asleep?" Detective Thompson asked Lisa, wincing as he wrapped gauze around his hand.

"She took a painkiller at three and was out by four," Lisa said.

He leaned against the counter, folding one long lean leg over the other. "How is she feeling? Has she been walking at all?"

Lisa turned to Jane. "If he hasn't told you, our mother had back surgery. And yes, she's doing much better now." She glared up at her brother. "If you were ever around, *Detective,* you would know that."

"I have a career."

"Yeah, well, so did I."

He snorted. "Washing *dogs*. That's not a career."

Lisa propped two combat boot-clad feet on the table. "Not *anymore*. And whose fault is that, you pompous ass?"

He leaned forward and shoved Lisa's feet back down. "Could you at least try to act civilized?" He turned to Jane. "Excuse my sister, her social skills are slightly lacking."

"And excuse my brother," Lisa said, her feet landing back on the tabletop with a loud thud. "He has a mild superiority complex. I had to give up *my* job to stay with *our* mother—who is driving me *insane*, by the way.

Would it kill you to take a day off every now and then and spend some time with her? I could use a break."

He leaned forward, lowering his voice. "And suppose she needed to use the bathroom or something. What would I do then?"

"*Help* her."

He looked mortified by the mere suggestion. "I can't do that. She's my mother."

"She's my mother, too, you moron," Lisa hissed. "You think this has been fun for me?"

"It's different. You're a girl."

She threw her hands up in frustration. "Ugh!"

Mitch slid into a chair and rubbed his bloodshot eyes. The poor guy looked exhausted. "Christ. I'll try to get some time off later this week, okay?"

"I saw you on the news," Lisa said. Though her tone was harsh, there was a distinct note of pride in her voice. "Did you get a confession?"

"We worked him over all night. Twelve hours and he didn't crack. When the news broke, and the family found out, they hired a lawyer."

"You look tired."

Mitch slumped down in the chair, his body slack. "I passed tired about eighteen hours ago."

"Why don't you leave your prisoner here. Go home and get some shut-eye." Lisa turned to Jane and winked. "If you're worried about her getting away, we can hand-cuff her to the table leg."

"Thanks, but I'm not letting her out of my sight."

"What, is she a dangerous criminal?" Lisa looked Jane over with mock scrutiny. "She doesn't look dangerous."

"She's *in* danger. Someone is after her, and I'm thinking it might be internal. So if anyone calls around looking for me, you don't know where I am."

"No kidding." Lisa sobered instantly, wearing the identical grim expression as her brother. "Where are you going to take her?"

"I was going to take her to a safe house, but considering recent developments, I'm not sure that would be such a good idea."

"What recent developments?"

"Getting shot at in an alley, for one. Someone knew we were going to be there."

Lisa's concern for her brother was clear on her face. Despite a major case of sibling rivalry, Jane could tell they were close. "Where will you go?"

"We'll stay in a hotel tonight."

"A hotel? What are you going to do, sit up all night guarding the door?"

"That's the plan," he said.

Jane drew up in her seat. The thought of spending the night in a hotel didn't exactly give her an overwhelming sense of security. If he was right, and someone on the force was a part of this, wouldn't it be easy for them to figure out where they were staying? And suppose he fell asleep? Who would protect her then? They would be like sitting ducks. "You can't sit up all night. You need rest."

"What I *need*," he said, "is to protect you."

That was just plain crazy. He couldn't stay awake *another* night. She flattened her palms on the table and prepared for a fight, which is what she knew it would take to change his mind. "I won't go."

His eyes darkened and his brow dipped low over his eyes. "You have to trust me."

"The hell I do when you're acting stupid. What if you fall asleep?"

"I *won't* fall asleep."

"But what if you do?"

"Jane—"

"*Mitch.*"

Her addressing him by his first name made his eyebrow quirk up. For a long moment they only stared at each other. "You know, you're not going to win this one."

"Why not take her to your house?" Lisa suggested.

Mitch and Jane simultaneously turned to look at her.

"Why his house?" Jane asked.

"Because it's about as secure as Fort Knox. You'd have to be Houdini to get into that place undetected."

"Oh, yeah, I'm sure that would go over big with my lieutenant," Mitch said. "There are certain rules I have to follow."

"So you can just leave that part out of your report. You can't deny it's the safest place you could take her. And you have a spare bedroom."

"That's beside the point." Mitch shifted uneasily. "It wouldn't be…appropriate."

"And your guarding me in a hotel room when you're compromised by lack of sleep would be?" Jane asked, hoping to appeal to that sense of responsibility and use it to her favor. The sharp look he shot her said she'd hit a nerve. "Admit it, Mitch. Staying at your place is a good idea. It's my fault that you were up most of last night."

"It wasn't your fault. I was doing my job."

"You were with her last night?" Lisa asked, her eyebrow lifting with curiosity—the same look Mitch had given Jane. She wondered if they knew how alike they looked.

"I was in the hospital," Jane told her. "He spent the night in the chair next to my bed."

"Awww," Lisa said. "That is *so* sweet."

"Ugh!" Mitch buried his head in his arms.

"That's nothing," Jane said. "When I was afraid to go into the bathroom alone, he went with me."

Lisa balanced on the back legs of the chair and folded her arms over her breasts. "Oh, so you'll take *her* to the bathroom, but not your own mother?"

Mitch lifted his head, glaring up at his sister. "I did not *take* her to the bathroom. I only stood in there while she looked in the mirror."

"And he looked at my butt," Jane told Lisa. "But only because it was hanging out the back of my gown, so it wasn't really his fault."

"Is that true?" Lisa asked Mitch. "You looked at this poor defenseless woman's butt?"

"He denied it at first, then when we were grocery shopping later he said—"

Mitch slammed a fist down on the table. "Enough already! You win. We'll stay at my house tonight. Jesus!"

Jane and Lisa shared a conspiratorial smile. That wasn't so hard. Mitch acted tough, but on the inside he was a big softie. And he'd been right about one thing. When Jane wanted something, she did get it.

Chapter 7

He'd been played, big-time, Mitch decided as he drove the three blocks to his house. He would have expected it from Lisa, but cute, innocent little Jane? *Innocent, my foot.* He should have known there was a shark lurking behind the sweet exterior. He should have realized her potential when she'd jumped out that window.

And though he hated to admit it, Jane was right. Another night without sleep and his reaction time would be grossly compromised. He couldn't risk that when her life could be at stake. He'd get a full eight hours tonight, then tomorrow night, if her memory still hadn't returned, he'd check them into a motel.

"What did Lisa mean when she called you a pompous ass?" Jane asked from the passenger seat. "And why would her lack of a career be your fault?"

He cringed at the thought of hashing out the ongoing battle between him and his sister. "It's kind of a long story."

"What, like I don't have time to kill?"

Mitch shot her a sidelong glance, recognized the determined look on her face, and sighed. Christ, she was a pain in the behind. Did she always have to be so difficult? "The short of it is, when our grandmother passed away, she left her house to Lisa and me. Lisa wants me to buy her half so she can open a dog grooming salon."

"Oh. Can you afford to do that?"

"Sure, I can afford it, but why would I sit back and let her throw her money away?"

"What makes you think she'll be throwing it away?"

"Lisa's no businesswoman. She barely graduated from high school and she only lasted a semester in community college. The idea has failure written all over it."

For a long moment the only sound in the car was the steady thrum of rain on the roof and the rhythmic thwack of the windshield wipers. He finally asked, "Should I interpret your lack of response as disapproval?"

"You really want to know what I think?"

Did he? In a way, he was curious, and at the same time, he was sure it would be in his best interest not to know. "I don't know. Do I?"

Jane turned to him, her expression thoughtful. "This is something she really wants to do?"

"It's all she talks about lately."

"And it is *her* money to spend?"

Okay, he could see where she was going with this.

"Technically, yes. But I control the estate. Lisa is horrible with money."

"Be that as it may, *technically,* the only thing stopping her from the career of her choice is you. Right?"

"I know how it sounds, but it's not that simple. You don't know Lisa. She's not exactly responsible. I mean, what if the business failed, what would she do then?"

"Hmm," she said, nodding.

"What, you think I'm being unfair?"

Her shoulders lifted in a casual shrug. "Obviously your mind is made up. Why should you care what I think?"

He made a left down his street. "I really do know what's best for her."

"I'm sure you do," she agreed.

He mumbled a curse under his breath. "Great, now you're making me feel guilty."

"If you're sure you're right, how could anything I say make you feel guilty?"

"Because you're agreeing with me to shut me up."

"If that's the case, it isn't working, because you're not shutting up."

"I can tell you think I'm wrong."

"What does it matter what I think? You know your sister better than anyone, right? As long as you're comfortable with your decision, no one else matters."

"I am. Very comfortable." As he pulled into his driveway, the security lights switched on, illuminating the interior of the car. "Is every female born with the ability to make a man feel like a heel or is that something they teach you in school?"

"Oh, please. What macho bull. 'Women have served all these centuries as looking glasses possessing the magic and delicious power of reflecting the figure of man at twice its natural size.'" She spouted the quote with as much authority as his women's studies professor in college. Then she frowned. "Wow. Where did that come from?"

"You just quoted Virginia Woolf," he said. "From *A Room of One's Own*."

"Did I? It just…popped out."

"That was interesting. I'd say it's safe to assume you've had some sort of college education." And that put an entirely new spin on the case. They'd been working under the assumption, considering her manner of dress and the contents of her shopping cart, that she'd been operating in a fairly low tax bracket. It was clear now—either she'd been educated, or was, at the very least, extremely well-read.

Or, God help him, a feminist.

"Anyone else you can quote?" he asked. "Thoreau? Dickinson?"

She shrugged helplessly, then glanced up through the windshield, as if noticing for the first time that they'd stopped. "This is your house?"

Mitch could swear she sounded a little apprehensive. Well, join the club. He wasn't entirely convinced this was a good idea. In fact, it had disaster written all over it. Yet he was too exhausted to argue the issue. And he didn't have the luxury of passing her off on someone else, not when he wasn't sure who to trust. "You're sure about this?"

She nodded. "I'm sure."

They both climbed out and she followed him to the porch. He unlocked the door, letting her into the foyer, where he switched on the light and punched the security code on the alarm to arm the system. If anyone tried to get in tonight, he would know about it.

Jane walked ahead of him into the living room. "Nice. Although, I never pictured you living in a house with flowered wallpaper and pastel chintz furniture. You must be awfully secure in your masculinity."

He took his jacket off and hung it on a hook by the door. "Not that secure. I just haven't had time to change much since I moved in."

He led her to the kitchen, dropping his keys and badge on the table. "Hungry?"

"I could eat," she said. "But would you mind terribly if I took a shower first? I'd really like to get the blood out of my hair."

He removed the clip from his Glock and set them both on the table beside his badge. "I'll give you the two-cent tour."

"I don't have two cents," she said, and he smiled.

"You can owe me."

He led her down a hall adorned with the same flowery print wallpaper to a bathroom decorated with so much bright yellow she had to fight the urge to shade her eyes. Despite the feminine touches the air was distinctly masculine, scented with aftershave and soap.

He gestured to the closet. "There are clean towels and I think there's a new toothbrush on the top shelf. Help yourself to whatever you need."

They crossed the hall to the spare bedroom. Decorated in dusty rose and leaf green, it was slightly less froofy than the rest of the house. A simple coverlet was draped over the queen-size bed and sheer white curtains hung in the window.

"The sheets are fresh and you'll find extra blankets and pillows in the closet."

Jane sat on the edge of the mattress, testing the springs. Lying back, she closed her eyes and sighed. "Ah, no lumps."

"I think Lisa has clothes in the closet. I'm sure she wouldn't mind if you borrow some. You look like you're about the same size."

"That would be great." She opened her eyes and sat up. Mitch stood in the doorway, arms folded over his chest, head resting against the doorjamb. He looked exhausted and rumpled and so adorable her heart warmed at the sight of him. He almost looked vulnerable, when she knew deep down he was anything but. "Thank you for letting me stay here. I know you could get in trouble for doing this."

He shrugged it off. "At least you'll be safe. While you take your shower I'll fix us something to eat. I think I have some lasagna in the freezer."

As if he hadn't done enough for her already. She should be cooking *him* dinner. That is, if she knew how. "Truthfully, I could go for something easy, like a tuna sandwich," she said, picking the first thing that popped into her mind. Hopefully she liked tuna.

He looked relieved. "Do you prefer white or wheat bread?"

She didn't have the slightest clue. "Surprise me."

"Take your time," he said, backing out of the room and closing the door behind him.

Jane stood and opened the closet. Several pairs of jeans hung there along with a few sundresses and a slew of T-shirts. She found one that looked large enough to pass as a nightshirt that read: *Heart attacks…God's revenge for eating his animal friends.* Lisa was obviously an animal lover.

Do I like animals? she wondered.

Was she a cat person? A dog person? Was she allergic? Did she have a pet when she was a kid?

Right, Jane. You can't remember your own children and you expect to remember a family pet. Way to keep those priorities straight.

Sighing, she pulled the shirt off the hanger and tossed it over her shoulder along with a flannel robe she found hanging on a hook on the back of the bedroom door. She searched the drawers of the dresser next, hoping to find a pair of underwear that might fit since hers had been cut off her at the hospital. If she'd learned one thing today, it was that denim chafed. Unfortunately, all the drawers were empty.

In the shower, she once again checked for stretch marks but couldn't find a single one. Her stomach was flat, her breasts high and firm, if not on the extremely small side.

She just couldn't accept that she had children. Natural or adopted. Or maybe the thought of her children, lonely and confused, waiting for her to return, was too much to bear. Why hadn't anyone come to claim her yet? Where was her family? Wasn't there anyone out there who loved or cared about her?

Sudden tears burned her eyes and she turned her face into the spray, rinsing them away. She'd come this far without totally losing it, she couldn't give in now. She had to trust that Mitch would figure this out—that they would solve it together.

Stepping out, she toweled off and dressed in the T-shirt and robe. She tugged the knots from her hair with a brush she'd found in the closet, then leaned close to the mirror and examined her teeth. They were perfectly straight and white, and if she had any cavities, they hadn't been filled with metal fillings. Would it be safe to assume a considerable amount of money had been invested in her mouth, or did she just have naturally strong and straight teeth?

She examined the greenish-purple bruises on both elbows and forearms, thankful she hadn't landed on her face instead. She found a few small scars she hadn't noticed before—a pale line about half an inch long above her right eyebrow, and a smaller scar at the corner of her right eye. Had an abusive husband done this to her, or had it been something as innocent as her falling off her bike as a child?

She frowned at her reflection. Scars, healed fractures…

Why hadn't she thought of that before?

A new surge of hope blossomed inside of her and she flung open the bathroom door. She found Mitch at the kitchen counter, preparing the sandwiches.

He turned toward her as she entered the room.

"I just realized something," she said. "I couldn't have an abusive husband. I must be divorced."

He carried two plates to the table, each with a sandwich, pickle wedge and a pile of potato chips. "How do you figure?"

"Besides my injuries from last night, I don't have a mark on me. All I have are old scars. If I were living with an abusive man, wouldn't I have recent injuries? If he were violent enough to break my bones, wouldn't I at least have bruises?"

He gestured to a chair, motioning for her to sit. "I thought about that."

She slid into her seat. "So you think it's possible?"

Jane looked so hopeful, Mitch hated to say anything to break her spirit. Still, he couldn't allow himself to reassure her with theories. "Anything is possible."

He started to sit, but the phone rang. He glanced over at the caller ID unit on the cordless phone. *Blocked.* If it was someone from the precinct or Lisa, it would have registered.

"Aren't you going to answer it?" Jane asked when he didn't move.

"Someone is purposely blocking the number," he said. "I want to see if they leave a message."

The machine picked up on the third ring, but when the tone sounded, there was a long drawn-out silence, then a click.

"It was him, wasn't it?" She paled and her steely gray eyes went wide. "He's looking for us."

"We don't know that for sure. It could have just been a wrong number or a telemarketer."

She didn't look like she believed that. He didn't mention that his number was unlisted, and obtaining it would have been difficult. Unless, of course, the suspect knew someone at the precinct. Or worked at the precinct. Even Mitch didn't want to think about the possibility of that.

Jane pushed her plate away. "I think I just lost my appetite."

"You're safe here. No one is getting past the alarm without me knowing about it." He wished there was some way he could erase her fear, her doubt. He reached across the table and slipped his hand over hers. Her skin was soft and warm but the tension in the muscles underneath clearly communicated her apprehension.

He gave her hand a reassuring squeeze. "I'm not going to let anything bad happen to you."

Their eyes met and the mood shifted. The air between them sparked with energy and the pace of his heart accelerated. Aw, hell. He never should have touched her, yet he couldn't seem to pull away. Jane was the one to tug her hand free, to break the spell.

She gave him a shaky smile. "I want to believe that."

But she didn't believe it. Her trust would have to be earned. He would have to prove that he could keep her safe.

"Why does a detective need a state-of-the-art alarm system anyway?" she asked, picking at the crust of her bread. "You'd have to be either really brave or really stupid to break into a cop's house."

Mitch was grateful for the neutral subject matter. "It's for insurance purposes. I have an extensive gun collection. It's been in my family for generations. A few date back to the Revolutionary War."

She nibbled on a chip. "What made you become a cop? Is that a family tradition, too?"

"My family has a strong military background. Everyone thought my dad would go career, but after one tour in Vietnam, he was through. He became a cop instead."

"Twin Oaks?"

Mitch nodded. "He took an early retirement when he got sick. Stomach cancer."

"When did he die?"

"It'll be three years next month."

She took a bite of her sandwich, chewing slowly. "And you've been taking care of your family ever since?"

"Pretty much."

She nodded. "Hmm."

He rolled his eyes. "Here we go again."

"What?" she asked, eyes wide and innocent. "I didn't say anything."

"You didn't have to." He finished his sandwich and carried his plate to the sink. "You're making those little disapproving noises again."

She gave him an honest to goodness laugh. "I am not."

"Are, too."

Jane placed her plate in the sink next to his. She'd barely touched her dinner. "I still contend that if you had nothing to feel guilty about, nothing I could say, no noise I could make, would make you feel that way."

He only grunted. She was right, of course. So why, he wondered, if he had nothing to be guilty about, did he feel so damned guilty anyway?

* * *

Mitch heard moaning.

At first he thought he was dreaming. In fact, he had been—about Jane. He dreamt she'd come to his room and crawled under the covers next to him. It was shadowy and disconnected, yet he had been acutely aware of her hands on his body. The moist heat of her mouth on his skin, her warmth against him, but when he'd reached for her he grasped only air.

"No!"

Mitch shot up in bed.

That was no dream. Tossing back the covers, he grabbed his Glock from the night-table drawer and rolled out of bed. How could anyone have gotten in? It would be impossible without triggering the alarm.

His heart thudding, he crept to the doorway. From there he could see into Jane's room, and though it took a moment for his eyes to adjust to the dark, he realized almost immediately that there was no one in there with her. If her thrashing and carrying on were any indication, he would guess she was having a nightmare.

The sudden rush of adrenaline abated and he sagged against the door frame. She was safe. For now, at least.

Watch it, Mitch. You're getting too close. Too involved.

Jane moaned loudly and mumbled in her sleep. He couldn't hear her clearly, but he could swear she said, "He took my baby."

Her baby? Glock at his side, he padded quietly across the hall to her room. She lay on her back wearing only a T-shirt, the covers kicked down to her feet. Though the shirt covered her to mid-thigh, it was still a lot more skin than he'd expected to see. It only served to remind him how long it had been since he'd had a woman in his house. In his bed.

Way too long.

She mumbled something he couldn't understand, and thrashed her head across the pillow.

"Jane." He grasped her shoulder and shook lightly. "Wake up, you're having a bad dream."

She batted at his hand and groaned, "No! Don't touch me!"

He ducked to avoid her flailing arm and grabbed hold of her wrist. "Relax, it's just me."

Her eyes flew open, wild and fearful, and before he knew what was happening, she sprang from the bed like a panther and they both went airborne. The gun flew from his hand, landed somewhere behind him and skidded across the hardwood floor. In the blink of an eye he found himself flat on his back, Jane straddling him, her forearm braced against his throat restricting his airflow.

He could have easily thrown her off—he should have thrown her off—but he didn't want to hurt her. "It's just me," he croaked.

She blinked several times as recognition set in, then gasped and jerked her arm away. "Oh, my God, are you okay?"

He rubbed his throat, swallowing a few times to make sure everything still worked. "Great. At least you didn't bite me this time."

Hands braced on either side of his head, she looked around, dazed. "How did I get down here?"

"You were having a bad dream," he said. "I tried to wake you up and you jumped on me."

"I did?"

"Where did you learn a move like that?"

"I don't know. Did I hurt you?" She raked her fingers through his hair, checking the back of his head, and every muscle in his body tensed. Her face was only inches from his, her sweet-smelling hair hanging down to tickle his cheek. It would be so easy to wrap his arms around her, pull her down. His mouth, her mouth…

For a moment he was immobilized by fear, fear that she might actually kiss him—or that she wouldn't. He closed his eyes and groaned.

"Mitch? Are you okay?" She shifted, rubbing him in just the right way, and a knot of pleasure tightened his groin. He instinctively grabbed hold of her hips to still her and wound up with two handfuls of smooth, bare skin.

Jane gasped, and for a moment they just stared at each other as if neither knew quite what to do next. Then she shifted again—deliberately this time, and probably to see how far she could push him.

At this point, not far. He sunk his fingers deeper into her flesh. "Don't do that again."

"Or what?" Through the darkness he could see the mischievous gleam in her eye, like she got a kick out of torturing him. And what a sweet torture it would be if he let it go any further. God help him, it was tempting as sin.

She cocked her hips again, creating more of that

sweet friction, and he bit his cheek to keep from moaning. She leaned down, until they were chest to chest, and whispered in his ear, "Is that a gun in your pants, or are you just happy to—"

The sound of shattering glass cut her short as the bedroom window exploded above them.

Chapter 8

Jane screamed and Mitch flung her over onto her back, shielding her from a shower of broken glass. The alarm wailed and the outside security lights blazed, streaming light through what was left of the sheer curtains. He heard another crash as the picture window in the living room was blown to smithereens.

Jane squirmed beneath him and he held her down with the full weight of his body. "Don't move," he hissed.

He scanned the floor for his weapon and discovered it lying several feet away, by the door. He cursed silently. A fat lot of good it would do him over there. There was too much glass on the floor to risk crawling over and grabbing it.

He lay perfectly still, watching the doorway for an intruder, becoming gradually, and painfully, aware of the woman lying beneath him. He caught the scent of his own shampoo and soap, yet it was distinctly feminine on her—sweeter, softer. Everything about her was soft. Soft breasts pressing against his chest, soft hair tickling his cheek, soft breathing in his ear. Their position should have been an uncomfortable one, yet they seemed to fit perfectly, like a key in a lock.

His key in her lock—if that wasn't an inappropriate euphemism, and not the kind of thing he should be imagining at a time like this. The arousal he had all but forgotten roared up inside of him with a vengeance. Thankfully Jane didn't perpetuate the problem by squirming around. She lay still beneath him.

After several minutes he raised up on his elbows, looking down at her. "You all right?"

She nodded, her eyes wide and fearful. "I think so."

"I think it's safe to assume your attacker knows we're here."

She clung to him, curling her fingers into his shirt. "What if he's still out there?"

"He's not. He would have found us by now. I think he was sending a message."

She looked up at the hole where the window used to be. "Not very subtle, is he?"

"And I'm sure we haven't heard the last of him."

The alarm ended abruptly and an eerie, all-encompassing silence followed. It was so quiet in the room, he could hear the steady thump of his own heart and the slightly faster beat of Jane's.

"What happened?" she asked, her voice filled with fear. "Why did it stop?"

"It's programmed to shut itself off after five minutes. The police are on their way."

Jane reached up and touched his arm. "Mitch, you're bleeding."

He looked down to see a stream of blood oozing from his forearm. It's a wonder they hadn't been cut to slivers. "It's just a scratch."

She raised up on her elbows, looking around them at the scattered shards of glass. The light shining through the window painted a treacherous path to the door. "How are we going to get out of here? There's glass everywhere."

"I hear sirens," Mitch said, cocking his head toward the window. They couldn't have been more than a mile away. "They'll be here any minute."

"Any minute?" She planted her palms against his chest and shoved, suddenly panicked. "We have to move. We can't let them see us like this."

"There's too much glass. Let's wait till help gets here."

"But, I'm not even supposed to be here! What will they think if they see us like…like *this*."

Yeah, what would they think? He had a pretty good idea. "I'm aware of how it looks."

"I don't think you are." She sunk her teeth into her bottom lip, a pained look on her face. "Mitch, I'm not wearing underwear."

He caught himself before he looked down. She had to be joking. "That's not funny."

"I'm not trying to be funny." She took his hand and guided it to her waist. "Do you feel a panty line?"

He slid his hand from her narrow waist, down her hip to one smooth—and completely bare—buttock. He yanked his hand away. "Christ, why didn't you say something?"

"I just did!"

"Why didn't you say something *before*?"

"Like what? 'Sorry I knocked you on your butt, Mitch, and oh, by the way, I'm not wearing panties.'"

The sirens were getting louder. They would be there any second. He wasn't worried so much about himself. He could handle the backlash he would catch if anyone discovered them this way. He was more concerned with how it would affect Jane. She'd been through enough in the past two days without dragging her into his personal problems. With his past experiences common knowledge among his colleagues, combined with her suspicious lack of underwear, no one would believe this to be completely innocent. Well, almost completely innocent. But before he could figure out a way to safely and discreetly climb off of her, he heard a noise across the room.

"I'm sorry," someone said from the doorway. "It looks like I've interrupted something."

"What the *hell* were you thinking?" Darren paced the kitchen like a caged animal. "You're just damned lucky I was on my way home when the call went out. If I hadn't gotten here first…damn it, Mitch, that was a stupid move."

Mitch looked over at Jane. She was still curled up in a blanket on the couch, talking to Officer Greene. She'd come through the event physically unscathed, while he'd suffered a few minor nicks on his arms and legs.

They were nothing compared to the lashing he'd been getting from Darren. "I told you already, it was completely innocent."

"Oh, yeah, the bad dream. I'm supposed to believe that a woman half your size somehow managed to disarm you and knock you on the ground? I'm not buying it."

"Okay, maybe my judgment was slightly compromised—"

"*Slightly compromised?* This is Kim all over again."

His statement drew several pairs of eyes their way, including Jane's.

"Look, I appreciate your concern, but there is *nothing* inappropriate going on."

"Don't you get it? This woman is playing you. She's a con artist."

Mitch knew Darren meant well. He was concerned for Mitch's well-being—his job. And he was only half wrong in his assumption—still it was difficult for Mitch to hold his temper. "If Jane had a criminal record, we wouldn't be standing here wondering who she is."

Darren didn't seem to hear him. Or didn't believe him. "What I can't understand is why you brought her here in the first place. She was supposed to be in a friggin' safe house across town."

"Someone is keeping tabs on me. Someone on the inside. I don't think she would have been safe there."

"Okay, now it's a conspiracy? Are we getting a little paranoid?"

Mitch wasn't even going to justify that one with a response.

"I have to file a report in the morning. How do you expect me to explain this?"

"You'll tell the truth and I'll deal with the consequences. Maybe I broke a few rules bringing her home, but I had her safety to consider."

"Her safety is worth your badge?"

"If doing my job to the best of my ability means taking risks, then yes."

"Damn it, Mitch, I can't stand by and watch you throw away ten years of service for some woman you don't even know. I *won't*. I'm going to recommend you're taken off the case."

Mitch pinched the bridge of his nose, taking a deep, calming breath. Exploding now would only make the situation more volatile. "Did you not hear a word I've said?"

"I've heard every word. I heard the same thing two years ago. If this woman means so little to you, why can't you pass the case over to someone else? No one will blame you for it."

"I told you, I need to solve this myself. She had *my name* in her pocket. I'm involved somehow. I need to know why."

Darren leaned against the counter, shaking his head. "Is it worth your career?"

"It won't come to that."

"One more incident, Mitch. You know they'll look for a reason. The D.A. is itching to nail you for something."

"That's why I have to know, why I have to solve this one myself. Am I attracted to her? Sure, who wouldn't be? Do I plan to do anything about it? Hell, no. I want to solve the case. That's it."

"Excuse me, Detective?" Officer Greene appeared in the doorway. "There's a call for you."

"Take a message."

"This can't wait. They need you at the hospital. There's been another attack."

They'd outsmarted him.

Rage seeped into his veins and the beast howled, bucking up against its chains. He was getting the urge again. Now that they had a suspect, he couldn't take the chance. Not without changing his MO. Even then it would be a risk. He was too smart to take risks.

It was rage that set the beast free the first time, rage that started the game. And his wife, the meddling bitch, she'd found his hiding place. She'd ruined everything. He should have put her in her place long ago. Always complaining, thinking she was smarter than him. Just like his mother.

He would show them. He was smarter.

Next time, he wouldn't fail.

Jane stood in the hall just outside of the emergency room, watching as Mitch spoke to the doctor on call. She was too far away to hear what was said, but by the solemn expressions they wore, she guessed the news wasn't good. Mitch listened intently to the doctor, jotting notes. He used the wall for support, looking bone-weary and frustrated. He'd been tight-lipped about the whole situation, though she had overheard that the victim had been attacked at the safe house that Mitch was supposed to have taken Jane to.

The doctor shook Mitch's hand and started down the hall, nodding in her direction as he walked past.

"Stay there," Mitch called to her before he disappeared behind one of the curtains separating the cubicles.

Though the smell alone was hauntingly reminiscent of her own hospital stay, and the thought of what she might see behind that curtain terrified her, she had to know what had happened. She had to hear and see it for herself.

The emergency room was fairly busy for 2:00 a.m. so she was able to follow him unnoticed. She stopped in front of the cubicle he'd entered and pulled the curtain back to see inside. Mitch stood with his back to her, blocking her view of the woman lying in the bed.

"What were you doing outside that late at night?" Mitch was asking her.

"Yeah," a gruff voice answered. "I tell you and you run to my probation officer. I don't think so, pretty boy."

"What's said here is off the record, between you and me. I'm investigating a case that might be related and I need your help."

There was a lengthy pause, then the woman said, "I needed a fix, okay? I had some stuff stashed behind the building. I bent over to look for it, and when I turned around there was some guy standing behind me. He shoved me back and smashed my head against the wall."

"Did you get a look at his face?"

"It was too dark, and he was wearing a hooded jacket. He was probably your height, maybe a little shorter. At first I thought my dealer sent him after me for testifying against him, but he smelled expensive."

There was another pause, then Mitch said, "What do you mean by expensive?"

"You know, like expensive cologne. He was clean."

Mitch jotted something in his notepad. "Did he say anything to you?"

"He asked me where his wife was," the woman said, and Jane's heart jumped into her throat. "He kept saying something like, 'You know where she is. Tell me where she is.' When I asked him his wife's name, he stopped, like he was confused or something, then he started wailing on me. He punched me a coupl'a times, and when I went down he started kicking me."

Mitch shifted to the left and Jane got an unobstructed view of the woman in the bed. Her left eye was blackened and swollen shut, her lip split and puffy, and a cast covered her left arm from shoulder to wrist. And those were only the visible injuries. She said he'd kicked her, too. She could have broken ribs, or internal bleeding. She could have *died*.

Jane's stomach rolled at the thought of the pain that poor woman must have endured.

That could have been me.

"Did he say anything else?" Mitch asked her.

"He said something about finding his kids. How she couldn't hide them forever."

Jane gasped, then slapped a hand over her mouth.

Mitch spun around, cursing when he saw her standing there. "I told you to wait in the hall."

"Is she the one he was looking for?" the woman spat. "Your husband is a lunatic, lady. Look what he did to my face."

Bile rose in her throat. Her husband, her kids? This couldn't be happening. "I'm so sorry," she whispered. "This is all my fault."

"If you remember anything else, call me," Mitch said, thrusting a business card at her. He grasped Jane's arm and ushered her from the room. "You didn't need to hear that."

"Yes, I did." She clasped her hands in tight fists, but couldn't stop them from shaking. "That should have been me. He was looking for me."

He pulled her aside and gripped her by the shoulders. "Listen to me, Jane. This isn't your fault. You couldn't have known he would do this. It's no one's fault."

"How could I be married to someone like that, how could I have children—" The words caught in her throat. "Is that what this is about? Did I hide our children? What if he finds them and hurts them?"

"We'll find them first."

"What if we don't?"

Mitch pulled her against him, wrapping his arms around her. She sank into him, pressing her cheek against his chest. How could she feel so safe in his arms, and at the same time, terrified and vulnerable? "I keep thinking it'll get better, that it'll be over soon, but it only gets worse."

With one arm draped protectively across her shoulders, Mitch led her to the emergency-room exit. "We both need sleep. Things will be clearer in the morning."

"Where are we going?"

"Back to my house."

"But—"

"No buts. It's still the safest place for you. The windows will be boarded up by now, and the alarm will cover every other possible entry point."

The air was crisp as they walked outside. She shivered under the light jacket and Mitch held her a little closer. "I heard what your friend said. I don't want to get you into any more trouble."

"You let me worry about Darren. Like I told him, my priority is keeping you safe."

"And if you can't keep me safe?"

He looked down at her, his eyes dark. "That's not an option."

Mitch woke with a start, springing up in bed, then he realized he wasn't in bed. He was on the bedroom floor. He rose up, squinted to see the digital clock.

Nine-thirty.

He looked up on the bed where he'd insisted Jane sleep, but it was empty. Then the scent of coffee and bacon registered in his fuzzy brain.

Yawning, he pulled himself up and stumbled to the bathroom. He unwrapped his hand, noting that it was healing well and didn't look infected. It still ached like hell though. He found a bottle of ibuprofen in the medicine chest and washed three down with water.

She'd proven in the alley and again last night, when it came to the fight-or-flight instinct, she was a fighter. Which was odd for a domestic-abuse survivor. Typically they were wary, afraid of people.

Nothing about this case seemed to add up.

He showered and brushed his teeth, and upon closer

inspection of his face, decided it was about time he shaved. After he dressed, he ventured out to see what Jane was up to. He found her in the kitchen, gazing out the window into the backyard, a cup perched in one hand.

"I thought you weren't a coffee drinker," he said.

She turned to him, her face unreadable. She looked neither surprised nor happy to see him. If anything, she looked a little lost. "It's tea. I made the coffee for you. Did you sleep well?"

He shuffled across the room to the cupboard and pulled out a mug. "Like the dead. How about you?"

She shrugged. Under her jacket she wore one of Lisa's old dresses, a flowery number made of a silky-looking fabric that hugged her narrow hips and swished around her legs as she crossed to the stove. Her hair was once again pulled up and fastened in a ponytail, showing off the long, graceful lines of her throat. Damn she was pretty.

Silently cursing himself, he looked away. After last night, it would be in his best interest to keep his eyes—and his hands—off of her today.

Jane slipped on an oven mitt and pulled a plate of bacon and a platter piled high with pancakes out of the oven. "Hungry?"

"Looks like you're planning to feed an army."

"I started mixing the ingredients and this is what I ended up with. I figured you could freeze the leftovers."

He watched as she set the plates down on hot pads and turned off the oven. "You didn't have to cook."

"It was a way to kill time."

"How long have you been up?"

Again with the shrug. "A few hours."

"We didn't get back here until almost three a.m. You must be exhausted."

"I slept enough." She pulled two plates down from the cupboard, and silverware from the drawer. It hadn't taken her long to familiarize herself with his kitchen. Not that he minded. He couldn't remember the last time he'd woken to find breakfast waiting for him. Kim, the only woman he'd ever lived with, had been a late sleeper. He'd realized too late that she'd existed on a pharmaceutical roller coaster—amphetamines to get her going in the morning and downers to knock her out at night. Oh, and he couldn't forget the occasional line of coke to help get her through the day.

"I, um, wanted to apologize for what happened last night," Jane said, as she dished the food onto the plates.

"I told you, there's no need to apologize. My insurance will cover the damage."

"Oh, I wasn't talking about the windows. I meant that I was sorry for knocking you down, and then, you know…*teasing* you. I don't know what got into me."

The mere thought of her teasing, and the realization that the only thing keeping them apart had been his boxers, filled his head with impure thoughts. The same things he'd been thinking last night, seconds before the windows had been blown out. It forced him to consider what would have transpired had there been no gunfire. In a moment of weakness would he have acted on those fantasies? Or would he have had the will to push her away?

To make matters worse, he was pretty sure she still wasn't wearing any panties.

"No harm done," he said. Nothing permanent anyhow. He was sure over time he would forget what her soft behind had felt like cupped in his palms. The silky, warm skin...

Okay, so maybe there was a little harm done. And it appeared to be manifesting itself in the region of his crotch.

"I cleaned up as much glass as I could in the living room and bedroom," she said. "I wanted to wait until you woke up to vacuum."

"You should have left it. I have a maid service that comes in and cleans once a week. I'll call and ask them to come by today." He grabbed the maple syrup from the fridge and followed her to the table, careful not to look anywhere south of her neck. They sat across from each other.

She didn't eat, only pushed the food around her plate with a fork. Something was definitely up with her. This wasn't the spunky, passionate woman he'd grown accustomed to. She was shutting down, turning in on herself.

"Are you okay?" he asked. "You're not acting like yourself."

"Like *myself*?" Her fork clattered to the table. "And how is that exactly? You don't even know who I am. *I* don't even know who I am. Did you ever consider that maybe this is normal for me."

"Jane—"

"I'm serious, Mitch." Jane pushed back from the table, the legs of the chair scraping loudly against the floor. "I could be anyone. I could be a thief. I could have been robbing you blind this morning and you never would have known. Why would you even trust me?"

"You didn't rob me blind. And if you were a known criminal, we would have found your prints in the database."

She raised her eyes heavenward and sighed. "You have an answer for everything, don't you?"

"I wish that were true. I wish I could tell you who you are, and why that man attacked you. And when I say you're not acting like yourself, I only meant you're tougher than this. You know that deep down."

"Oh, yeah?" She fidgeted with the zipper on her jacket, glancing up at him through a veil of thick, dark lashes. "I wasn't so tough when I was throwing up on you."

He shook his head and smiled. "You'll never let yourself live that one down, will you?"

"I'll bet you never did."

"No, but I have gotten sick at crime scenes. Everyone has their physical and psychological limits. Sometimes even seasoned cops get sick. It reminds you that you're human, that you still have feelings."

She was quiet for a minute, the hint of a smile nudging up the corner of her mouth. "How do you do it?"

"Do what?"

"You always manage to say just the right thing. You make things seem less…hopeless."

He reached across the table and took her hand. What he really wanted to do was hold her. "Because things aren't hopeless, Jane. Not yet, anyway."

Chapter 9

Jane looked down at Mitch's hand curled over hers, then up into his eyes and her heart jumped into her throat. His eyes were so full of compassion, she went fuzzy and warm inside. Despite this whole mess, at that moment, she felt inexplicably safe. "Thank you."

He gave her hand a squeeze and pulled away. "I do have to be honest with you. We have a dozen pieces to this puzzle, but none of them seem to fit together. I've got Greene working on it, but until someone reports you missing, or you get your memory back, I'm out of ideas."

"And he'll keep stalking me."

"But he won't get you. I won't let that happen."

She had a sudden revelation. An idea so crazy, it just might work. And for the first time that morning she felt enthusiastic. Hopeful even. "Maybe you should."

"Should what?" He stood and carried his plate to the sink.

"Let him get me. He gets me, and you get him."

He turned to her, eyes widened with disbelief. "Are you suggesting that I use you as *bait?*"

"You said that he could have killed me if he wanted to, that he needs something from me. I know it sounds nuts—"

"It doesn't just *sound* nuts, it is nuts."

"Like you said, I'm tough. I can handle it. I think it would work."

"Absolutely not."

"But, Mitch—"

"*No.* It's not even up for discussion. What he did to that woman last night, that was pure rage. What if I didn't get to you in time?"

"You would."

He shook his head. "No way. I'm not willing to take that risk. If it were my own life at stake, it would be different."

One minute he says she's tough, then he's back to coddling her. She wished he would make up his mind. Or maybe she would have to make up his mind for him. Would it be so hard to plan something all by herself? She would have to sneak away from him somehow, but not so far that he wouldn't be able to get to her in an emergency. She would have to act quickly, when the opportunity presented itself.

Jane followed Mitch to the sink, setting her plate beside his, the wheels in her mind spinning—devising a plan.

"Uh-oh," Mitch said.

She looked up, startled. "What? What's wrong?"

His brow sunk low. "Don't even think about it."

"About what?"

"You're planning something. I can see it in your eyes. You looked exactly like this when I dropped you off at the halfway house yesterday."

"That's ridiculous," she said, avoiding his eyes. How could he possibly know what she was thinking? Could she be that transparent?

She opened the dishwasher and began stacking the dirty dishes inside. She would have to be more careful from now on. She'd figured from the start that he was a good detective. Maybe a little too good. His instincts were always right on the mark.

"Promise me you won't," he said from behind her.

He was so close, she jolted with surprise and spun to face him. "Won't what?"

He curled his fingers around her arm. "I mean it, Jane. Promise me you won't pull some crazy stunt and get yourself hurt."

If there was any doubt before that he cared for her, at that moment, it was evident in his eyes. That didn't change the fact that she wanted answers. Still, she couldn't very well make him a promise she knew she wouldn't keep.

She chose her words with care. "Nothing crazy. I promise."

"But you are planning something, aren't you?" He had her cornered, her back pressed against the edge of the countertop, his hand clasped about her forearm—

firmly enough to let her know he meant business, but not with enough force to inflict pain. And he was close. Close enough for the flesh on the back of her neck to prickle, close enough to catch the faintest scent of coffee on his breath—

"Tell me the truth," he coaxed, locking her deep into his gaze. She cursed those magnetic eyes of his. They hypnotized, willed her to confess.

He learned in closer, until they were almost nose to nose. "Tell me the second I turn my back you won't disappear on me."

He was wearing her down. It took every ounce of willpower she could muster to keep her mouth closed. What she needed was a diversion. If only the phone would ring, the doorbell chime…the house burst into flames.

He moved closer still, insinuating one leg between her two, his body molding to hers. He wasn't playing fair. They were locked from hip to chest, the only sound, her own heart hammering wildly against her rib cage, the rasp of her breath as she fought to keep a hold of her wits. He reached up and cupped her cheek and her knees went wobbly. Then there *were* flames. Embers smoldered deep inside her. The promise of…of what? Hot sex they would both regret. It would be immeasurably stupid.

Of course, it didn't have to be sex. It could be a kiss. One harmless little kiss. Then she wouldn't continue to wonder what she was missing. Hell, it might not even be any good. He could be a lousy kisser. She would never know if she didn't give it a test run.

"Oh, what the hell." She flung her arms around his neck, lifted up on the tips of her toes and pressed her lips to his.

There was an instant of hesitation on his part, then his lips softened and he leaned into the kiss. She felt his hands cupping her cheeks, his fingers slipping through her hair. He tilted her head, deepening their contact. At the first touch of his tongue against her own, as their breath mingled, the world went blurry around the edges. What started out sweet and gentle quickly became urgent—demanding even. He held nothing back. He kissed with an honesty that blew her away. It curled her toes and liquefied her bones and turned everything else to putty.

He possessed her—owned her. And just when she began to lose herself completely, when the last of her apprehension slipped away and it was just her and Mitch, the phone rang.

He surprised her again by backing off slowly, hesitantly, his lips lingering against hers for several seconds before he finally pulled away. She'd expected him to dart back, cursing himself for his actions—for his mistake—but he didn't let her go. He only sighed, eyes closed, and rested his forehead against hers.

"I should get that," he said, but didn't seem to be in a hurry to move.

"It could be important," she agreed, dropping her arms from around his neck.

He reached over her and grabbed the phone. "Yeah."

He listened for several minutes, nodding his head and responding with an occasional, "Uh-huh."

Considering the grim expression on his face, she guessed it wasn't a social call. She laid her head against his chest, feeling the vibration of his voice against her cheek. If only the kiss had been lousy. She would have even settled for so-so. Instead it had to be wonderful. Amazing.

Perfect.

"Yes, sir, Monday morning," he said, then pushed the disconnect button and set the phone down on the counter.

"Problem?" she asked

He linked his arms around her back, resting his chin on the top of her head. "My lieutenant."

"Are you in trouble?"

"He didn't sound happy, but he told me to sit tight until tomorrow morning. He trusts me."

Guilt assailed her. How would his lieutenant feel had he known she and Mitch had been playing tonsil hockey when he'd called? That if he hadn't called at that particular moment, the situation would have progressed to something a hell of a lot more intimate than a kiss.

"I'm sorry," she said.

"You know, you spend an awful lot of time apologizing for things that aren't your fault."

"I shouldn't have kissed you."

He smoothed his hands over her shoulders. "It was that bad, huh?"

She sighed and closed her eyes. "I wanted it to be. I wanted it to be awful, but it wasn't. It was a slice of heaven. But I'm just going to get you into more trouble."

"So why did you do it?"

"I needed a diversion."

A laugh rumbled through his chest. "It worked."

"We shouldn't do it again. At least, not until we know who I am."

"I know." After one last squeeze, he pulled away. "I do have a favor to ask."

She drew her arms around herself, to ease the emptiness she felt the instant he'd pulled away. "Anything."

"Trust me. Trust that I'm damn good at what I do, and I won't let you down. It may take some time, but we will figure this out. And we'll do it together."

A sudden surge of emotion had tears welling in her eyes. "I wish I knew why it's so hard for me to trust you. To trust anyone. But I want to be in control. This feeling of helplessness is making me nuts."

"And it makes me nuts that you won't let me take care of you. I don't want you to get hurt." He brushed a wayward tear from her cheek with his thumb—which only brought her closer to a meltdown.

"Look what you're doing to me," she said with a sniffle. "Stop being so nice."

"Promise me you won't try anything."

She huffed out an unsteady breath. "If you're not careful I'm going to need another diversion."

He cradled her chin in his palm, forcing her to look at him. "Go ahead and kiss me again if you have to. I'm not letting this go until you promise me."

It was tempting. Kissing him again, that is. Because he did it so well. Which is precisely why she didn't. The next time they wouldn't stop with a kiss. On the off chance that she was some sort of criminal, or someone's wife, and out of respect for Mitch, she couldn't let it happen. "So what if I do promise? How do you know I won't just turn around and do it anyway?"

"Because I trust you."

That one just about did her in. And as badly as she wanted to, she couldn't tell him no. She couldn't deceive him. "Fine," she said, pulling her chin away. "I promise. Sheesh! Are you happy?"

He only grinned, and seeing him so pleased suddenly made the sacrifice worthwhile. And that scared the hell out of her. When had his happiness become so important to her? If there was ever a time to be selfish, it was now.

Old habits, a little voice in her head sang before the memory was swallowed up again.

What old habits?

"Is something wrong?" Mitch asked. "You just got a funny look on your face."

"Fleeting memory," she said, giving her head a shake to clear away the bitter aftereffect. "Whatever it was, it's gone now."

The phone rang again and he scooped it off the counter. He spoke briefly to the caller before hanging up. "We have to make a stop at the precinct. Greene thinks he may have found something."

A burst of hope and anxiety bloomed inside of her. "Does he know who attacked me? Does he know who I am?"

"He didn't say exactly, but it sounded urgent." He snapped up his badge from the counter. "This could be the break we've been waiting for."

* * *

"What have you got for me?" Mitch asked, sliding into his chair. Jane perched on the corner of his desk, while Greene, the eager young officer who had questioned her last night, dropped a thick folder in front of Mitch.

"I pulled the file on last night's victim," he said. "Something just didn't sit right with me about the attack."

"Yeah," Mitch agreed. "I had that feeling, too."

"Take a look at her file. Her height, her hair."

Mitch opened the file, read for several minutes, then said, "I'll be damned."

"What is it?" Jane asked.

Mitch rotated the file to give her a better look. "Same hair color, similar build."

Jane studied the photo, her breath catching when she realized what he was implying. "You think she looks like me?"

"Not in the face. But she said he came up behind her. It's possible that in the dark, the suspect could have mistaken her for you."

"If he mistook her for me…" Honest to goodness hope swelled to the surface in a rush so powerful it choked her up. "Does that mean…?"

"He was asking *you* where his wife is. Which would mean this guy isn't your husband."

"Which also means I probably don't have children hidden somewhere, scared and missing me. I didn't forget my own kids." That was the biggest relief of all. But it was short-lived.

"If that's true, it could also mean that you probably

know where *his* wife and kids are. Or at least he thinks you do."

Officer Greene cleared his throat. "Um, if you don't need me for anything else, Detective, I'd like to head home and spend some time with my kids."

Mitch stood. "Yeah, sorry. Thanks for calling me in."

"No problem." With a shy smile, Greene tipped his head in Jane's direction, "Ma'am."

"He's nice," Jane said when he was gone. "And so young. He doesn't look old enough to have kids."

"He's a good cop," Mitch said. "A good guy."

She looked over at him, brow furrowed. "Who is Kim?"

Her shift of subject stunned him for a second. "How do you know about Kim?"

"Arnold Palmer mentioned her last night."

Arnold Palmer? Now he had to wonder if that bump on her head had done some damage after all. "Arnold Palmer? The golf pro?"

"You know, your friend in the golf clothes. The other detective. He said that I was Kim all over again. What did he mean by that?"

Mitch sat back in his seat, suppressing a chuckle. Darren did dress preppy. Very clean-cut. "Kim was a woman I was seeing a few years back."

"Seeing?"

"Living with."

"Is she the one you almost married?"

"I thought about it."

"And exactly how does that compare with you and me?"

He shifted uncomfortably. "It's, uh, kind of ironic, actually."

She leaned forward. "Why do I get the feeling you mean ironic in a bad way?"

"I was working narcotics at the time. Kim's boyfriend was dealing. When she found out, she turned him in to the police. He rolled on his suppliers and she agreed to testify, so we placed her in protective custody as a precaution."

"Let me guess. You were assigned to her case."

He nodded. "You know what they say about hindsight. I was still pretty upset over losing my dad and she used that as a way in. Looking back, I can see that she manipulated me. Darren could see it, too, and he tried to warn me."

"But you didn't listen."

"Kim and I had been together about three months when she was busted for possession. All the signs were there. I just didn't want to see it."

"Is she in jail?"

"No," he said, voice flat, eyes devoid of emotion. "She's dead."

Jane shuddered involuntarily and shivers crawled up her back. "Drug overdose?"

"She was murdered."

"Was it because of the drugs?"

"I'll never know for sure. We never found out who did it."

She wanted to touch him, to offer some gesture of comfort, but knew how it would look. "I'm so sorry, Mitch. That must have been awful."

"And it got worse. It wasn't until after she died that I found out she was married."

"Ouch."

"Yeah. Ouch. Makes a person wonder why I kissed you this morning."

"You didn't kiss me," she said. "I kissed you."

"But I let you."

They had one of those moments where their eyes locked and held and she had the unmistakable feeling that he could see deep inside of her. She couldn't help wondering what he saw there. Then her temperature started to rise, and her mind began to wander back to their kiss.

Looking away, Mitch cleared his throat and unfolded himself from the chair. "We should go."

Jane resisted the urge to fan away the flames that had settled in her cheeks. "Yeah. I could use some fresh air."

Outside, the sun shone brightly overhead and heat poured in waves off the surface of the blacktop. She caught the sweet fragrance of the lavender that grew in thick clusters around the building, their branches heavy with hearty purple blooms.

They walked through the near deserted parking lot to the sedan. He closed her door and walked around to the driver's side, snagging a flyer from the windshield as he got in. He unfolded the paper, his brow dipping into a deep furrow as he read. His expression grim, he looked up, glancing around the parking lot.

"What's wrong?" Jane asked.

Mitch held the paper up. There were two words typed across the page: *I'm watching*.

"It's from him," she said, shivering despite the heat.

"He's trying to scare you." He tucked the paper into his jacket pocket.

"It's working. Shouldn't you check it for prints?"

"He didn't leave prints. He's smarter than that." He started the engine and turned to her. "Do you trust me?"

"I do," she said with a certainty she hadn't felt since this whole mess began. She'd be a fool not to. "I trust you."

"Good. Then you know that I'm not going to let him get you. He may be smart, but I'm smarter."

His cell phone began to ring and he answered with his usual, "Thompson." He listened for several minutes then expelled a stream of obscenities she'd never imagined coming out of his mouth.

"I'm on my way." He stabbed the Off button and turned to Jane. "Buckle up."

Throwing the car into gear, he peeled out of the parking lot.

His sudden shift in demeanor was as thrilling as it was frightening. She'd seen him in cop mode before, but never like this.

"We have to make a stop at the county lockup," he said, taking a corner at excessive speed.

Jane realized, by his clipped tone, he wasn't just in cop mode. He was furious. "What's wrong?"

"I made an arrest two days ago. A serial rapist named Robby Barrett."

"The one you interrogated all night?"

"That's the one."

"Did he confess?"

"No. They found him hanging in his cell this morning."

Chapter 10

"How in the *hell* did this happen?"

"He tore his clothes apart, made a rope and hung himself." The D.A. sat in a massive leather chair, behind an equally massive desk—a desk meant to convey his powerful position no doubt, yet he looked anything but. He looked tired, bored even.

Mitch on the other hand was livid. Jane watched from the doorway as he leaned forward, resting both hands on the desktop, getting in the man's face.

"So what you're telling me is that he tore his clothing apart, managed to tie it all together in a handy rope, hung himself from the bars of his cell and *no one* noticed?"

"You got your arrest, Detective. You had your moment in the spotlight. Let it go."

"I didn't get my confession."

"He was *guilty*. I prefer to think that he did us a favor. He saved the taxpayers the expense of a trial and incarceration."

"Will you be including that in your press release?"

The D.A. sat forward, his tone threatening. "Let it *go*, Detective."

Mitch didn't back down. If anything, he crept farther into the other man's personal space. "There is the matter of a man being innocent until proven guilty. He deserved a fair trial."

"Which he would have gotten if he hadn't taken his own life."

Mitch started to turn away, his jaw rigid.

"One more thing, Detective. The family has already contacted a lawyer. Not only do they want vindication of his death, they want to prove his innocence." The D.A. stood. He was a formidable presence, towering a good three inches over Mitch. "It's likely you'll be subpoenaed to testify. I'm counting on your cooperation in the matter."

No threat was voiced, but the implication was clear. Many men would have been intimidated. Mitch didn't bat an eyelash. And for some silly reason it filled her with pride. He was truly one of the good guys.

"Always a pleasure," Mitch said, extending one arm for a brusque handshake. The level of hostility in the gesture was so intense she could practically feel the surge of testosterone. Then Mitch turned and headed for the door, hooking a hand under her elbow and leading her into the hall, muttering under his breath, "Smug son of a bitch."

She practically had to run to keep up with him. "He didn't just ask you to lie under oath, did he?"

"Of course not," he ground out through clenched teeth. "He's a D.A. He would never direct a witness to lie."

"But he would imply it?" When he didn't answer, she said, "You two had quite a rapport going in there."

"Let's just say that we have a history." He stopped in front of the elevator and punched the Down button. The halls were deserted; still he lowered his voice. "When the whole Kim thing went down, he was a prosecutor. He was convinced I was involved and dead set on nailing me. It was a failure he's obviously not taken in stride."

"He thought you were involved in drugs?"

"No. In her murder."

"You're a cop. Why would he think that?"

"When someone is bludgeoned to death in your apartment, they tend to look at you as a suspect." He slammed the palm of his hand against the button again. "And no, I didn't do it."

"I would never believe you could do something so awful," she said softly. "Why would they think…"

"We had a pretty major blowout over her arrest. I bailed her out, then gave her an hour to pack her things and get out of my apartment. I left, drove around for a while to cool down, and when I came back an hour later, she was dead."

"And this D.A. still thinks you did it?"

"He doesn't care about guilt or innocence. He's a damned politician. He only cares about winning."

"You were great in there. I know it probably sounds stupid, but I was proud of you for not backing down."

"Another minute and he would have been eating my fist." He stabbed the button again, and when the doors didn't open, he latched back onto her arm and tugged her down the hall and through the door leading to the stairs.

Mitch let go of her arm and started down, halting when he realized she wasn't following him. He looked back at her questioningly. She leaned against the door, looking at him in the oddest way.

"What?" he asked.

"It was a turn-on."

For a second he was sure he'd misunderstood. "I beg your pardon?"

"Watching you in there. Knowing you were fighting for what you believe in. It was…intense."

"And it turned you on?"

She flattened her palms against the door behind her. "Oh, yeah. Big-time."

Okay, maybe he hadn't heard her wrong. He could distinctly see color climb up her neck and flame out onto her cheeks. He could see the heavy rise and fall of her breasts with every breath.

He took a step toward her, knowing he shouldn't get any closer. Though it was obvious, he asked anyway, "You're turned on right now?"

She nodded.

"Let me guess, you're one of those danger types? Being in peril gets you hot?"

She shrugged. "I don't know. Maybe I am."

He should just shut his mouth, turn around and run as far and fast as he could in the opposite direction. At least until they'd both had a chance to cool down. But damn it, he couldn't. Instead of walking away from her, he stepped closer. "You know, that honesty thing you have going is bound to get you in trouble one of these days."

"Is that a threat, Detective?"

It happened so fast, he couldn't say for sure who moved first. One minute they were three feet apart, the next she was in his arms. He backed her against the door, pinning her with the weight of his body, fueled by his anger and frustration. Lips crushed and molded, tongues collided. She was like an oasis, so sweet and hot, he thrust to taste her deeper. She responded with equal enthusiasm, bearing her soul to him right there in the stairwell.

Like magic, the hostility that had consumed him only seconds earlier began to drain away. A satisfying, mellow kind of heat that started in his chest spiraled outward in a slow rush, like warm honey in his veins. And though he was sure there were several dozen reasons why making out in the county courthouse was probably a lousy idea, he couldn't conjure up a single one.

She tugged his shirt from the waist of his jeans, smoothed her hands across his bare stomach and up his chest, and he came up with several dozen reasons why it was a *pretty good* idea—the soft gasp she let out when he molded his hand over the swell of her breast, the fingernails raking a path down his back. Very good reasons.

It also became clear that if either of them didn't come to their senses soon, there was a strong possibility they would wind up making love right there against the door. And while personally he didn't consider their actions reprehensible—with the possible exception of public in-decency—he was somewhat convinced his superiors would frown upon his behavior. At the very least he could count on a formal reprimand. And call it an over-active sense of morals, but he couldn't brush aside the idea that, given the nature of their relationship, he was somehow taking advantage of Jane.

Ultimately, that sense of justice she'd found so arous-ing was what continued to keep them apart.

He pulled away slowly, letting that final kiss linger as long as possible. "We can't."

She rested her cheek against his chest. "I know."

He circled his arms around her, unwilling to let go just yet, surprised to find that simply holding her filled some void he hadn't even realized was there. Until he'd found her sprawled out in that store, until he'd gotten to know her, to appreciate her quirky personality, he'd been…lonely. Christ, for the first time in years he felt like a whole person again. And the woman who made him feel that way could be damn near anyone.

"We can't let this happen again." He smoothed back the hair that had come loose from her ponytail. Try as he might, he just couldn't seem to make himself stop touching her. "Not until we know who you are."

She looked up at him, her eyes full of hope. "And after we know who I am?"

"Realistically…"

"It would still be a bad idea," she finished for him, her voice filled with a finality that cut deep.

"I was going to say, you have a life somewhere that I might not fit into."

"It's odd. We've only known each other two days but I feel like we've been friends my whole life."

"In a way, these past two days have been your whole life." Which didn't explain why he was feeling exactly the same way. "It wouldn't be fair to either of us if we were to get involved now."

"You're right," she agreed, backing away. She was trying to be strong, but he could see the hurt in her eyes. Though it was difficult now, in the long run they would both be better off. She would thank him.

That didn't make letting go any easier.

"Where to now?" Jane asked when they were in Mitch's car.

"I thought we could drive around for a while, see if anything triggers a memory."

"What about your sister?"

He started the engine and steered out of the nearly empty lot. "What about her?"

"Weren't you supposed to get those groceries for her?"

"I'm working."

She gave him a "yeah right" look.

"If I go over there, I'm going to get sucked into doing something else. She keeps lists, for cryin' out loud."

"Lists?"

"Grocery lists, chore lists. She's ruthless."

"But you promised. And she is the one who gave up her job to stay with your mother."

She was right and he knew it. He cursed and punched the gas, sending them shooting out into traffic.

"Fine, we'll get the damned groceries," he mumbled. "But that's it. We drop them off, then we leave."

With a grin on her face, Jane watched out the open kitchen window of his mother's house while Mitch trudged the length of the yard behind a lawnmower. Proving yet again that, though he tried to act tough, he was a big softy. It had taken minimal pouting and a few veiled threats for Lisa to get him out there.

It wasn't like she and Mitch had anything better to do. Well, that wasn't exactly true. They could be out driving around, looking for something familiar. Yesterday it was all she wanted to do. Now, the thought left her feeling vulnerable. And…alone. Mitch had barely spoken to her when they picked up Lisa's groceries. She figured it was his way of putting distance between them, of trying to forget what happened in that stairwell.

She couldn't imagine spending the entire day that way. In an awkward, uncomfortable silence.

Here, at least she had Lisa to talk to. Lisa, who'd been stuck in the house for weeks taking care of her mother and seemed to need the company as badly as Jane did. And just as it had been with Mitch, Jane felt some sort of connection to Lisa. A kinship.

A warm breeze kissed her face and the scent of freshly cut grass washed over her like a long lost friend. It was so familiar—comforting even—but any distinct memory escaped her. Rather than let frustration set in, she instead watched Mitch. With the temperature steadily creeping up and the noon sun beating relentlessly down, he'd abandoned his shirt on the picnic table. She watched the lean muscle in his shoulders bunch and contract under sweat-slicked skin, his powerful legs flex under denim. She couldn't peel her eyes away. Which was probably why she didn't hear Lisa come up behind her and let out a shriek when she tapped Jane's shoulder.

"Something interesting out there?" Lisa asked, a mischievous grin on her face.

Jane had been caught red-handed staring—a denial seemed futile. "I think I'm falling for your brother."

Lisa looked a bit taken aback by her honesty, but she smiled. "He's a good guy. When he takes his head out of his ass."

"He thinks we shouldn't start anything. At least until we know who I am. Not that I blame him." She let out a sigh so long and wistful she turned her own stomach. "God, I'm pathetic."

"I hate to be discouraging, but when he sets his mind to something, he's tough to budge."

"So I've noticed."

"You know he's been burned pretty badly before."

She nodded. In the yard, Mitch stopped briefly and drew one tanned arm across his sweat-soaked brow. Her thoughts drifted back to their encounter in the stairwell. She recalled how all of that lean muscle, that warm smooth skin, had felt against her palms. A deep sense of longing took a choke hold of her heart. "He told me about Kim. The crazy thing is, I don't know that I'm any different. Suppose I am caught up in something illegal. Suppose I'm on the run from someone."

"If it's any consolation, you don't look like a criminal."

"I don't feel like a criminal either, but that doesn't mean I'm not."

"Kim, she was…I don't know, *shifty*, I guess. She was sticky sweet to Mitch, but when he wasn't around, she was an ice cube. I never believed that she loved him." Lisa boosted herself up to perch on the edge of the countertop. The tank top she wore today read: All Men Are Animals, Some Just Make Better Pets. "He got a lot of flack from her family after she was killed. Her husband blamed Mitch. He went to Mitch's lieutenant and the police chief, and when they wouldn't listen, he went to the newspapers. It was a huge mess. He almost lost his job."

"And now he doesn't trust women. I really can't say I blame him. Especially a woman like me."

"You're different, Jane. I can tell."

"I appreciate that. But it doesn't change the fact that this thing between me and Mitch will never work."

"I kinda think of it like this—Mitch keeps a pretty high wall around himself, and it's not very often he lets people in. Right now you're on the top of that wall, your feet dangling over the edge, waiting for the go-ahead to jump down so he can catch you."

"And if I jump down without waiting for permission?"

"You risk landing on your ass."

That was pretty much the conclusion she'd drawn, as well. And it wasn't a risk she was willing to take. Not yet anyway. "Tell me about this dog-grooming shop you want to open."

Surprise and excitement sparked in Lisa's eyes. "Mitch told you about it?"

"Not in detail."

"It's more than a dog-grooming shop. It's a pet resort, and not just for dogs. Cats, birds, hamsters—any animal is welcome. We would have grooming services, exercise programs, gourmet food, an on-call veterinarian. You name it."

"It sounds really unique, but is there a market for that kind of thing?"

"I never thought so, but I have this friend who owns a resort up near Traverse City. Very exclusive. He caters to the filthy rich and eccentric, and a lot of them bring their pets along. He approached me about the possibility of adding a grooming salon, so I told him about my pet resort idea. He loved it! Unfortunately, David can only afford to put up half the money and he's having a little trouble talking his investors into shelling out the rest. If I'm going to make this work, I need to come up with the second half myself."

"Your half of your grandmother's house," Jane said, and Lisa nodded. "Maybe if you try to reason with Mitch—"

"You can't reason with Mitch. I admit, I haven't exactly been the poster child for responsibility, but this resort is what I've *always* wanted to do. It's the only thing I've ever felt passionate about."

That passion was evident in Lisa's face. How could Mitch be so blind to his own sister's enthusiasm? Jane didn't doubt that he meant well—or that he had a grossly inflated sense of responsibility where his family was concerned. But Lisa deserved the chance to try. *Everyone* deserved the chance to try. Even if that meant falling on their face a time or two.

From the open window she heard the lawnmower cut out and glanced up to see Mitch drop down onto the picnic table, sprawling across the top on his back, one forearm draped over his eyes.

Maybe it would be the opportune time to talk some sense into him. When his defenses were down.

"He looks thirsty," Jane said.

Lisa hopped down and looked over Jane's shoulder, out the window. "You think?"

Jane nodded. "Definitely. We wouldn't want him to dehydrate."

"Nope, that would be bad. Maybe you should bring him something to drink." Lisa reached into the refrigerator and pulled out a pitcher of lemonade. She filled an oversize plastic cup and dropped in a few ice cubes. With a cocky smile she shoved the cup into Jane's hand. "Go get him, tiger."

Chapter 11

Mitch sighed, the weathered wood of the old picnic table rough against his back, the sun searing his bare chest and arms—but he was too relaxed to move a muscle. The hum of an occasional insect buzzing past his ear and the trill of a bird in the trees lulled him deeper into a state of unconsciousness. Even when he heard the creak of the back door, sensed the rustle of footsteps crossing the lawn, he was helpless to open his eyes. Still, before she uttered a sound, he instinctively knew it was Jane. Every other one of his senses told him so. The scent of her hair, the sound of her breathing and the unmistakable tingle of awareness across his skin.

"Sleeping on the job?" she asked, making a "tsk, tsk" sound. The table tilted slightly to one side as she took a seat on the bench. "You looked thirsty, so I brought you lemonade."

He lifted his arm a fraction of an inch and peeked at her through one half-shut eye. "You might have to feed it to me intravenously. I can't move."

"One strategically placed ice cube and I bet I could have you off that table in a millisecond."

The mischief in her tone warned him that she would probably make good on the threat. With a groan he shoved himself up, rubbing his eyes with a thumb and forefinger. When he finally focused on her, and got an eyeful of bare skin, he snapped awake instantly. She'd taken off her jacket and the dress she wore hung by two narrow straps of fabric. The naked skin of her shoulders looked translucent in the sunshine and her pale hair shimmered like gold dust. He didn't have to imagine what that skin felt like, the way it slipped like warm satin beneath his fingers, and he itched to relive the experience all over again.

She held the glass out and he took it, their fingers touching for only an instant, but it was long enough to send a shock wave of sensation up his arm.

"Thanks," he said, taking a gulp of the icy liquid— when what he should have done was dump it over his head. "I'm almost finished with the lawn."

"No hurry." She drew one leg up and rested her chin on her knee. "I was hoping we would still be here when your mom wakes up. I'd like to meet her."

"I'm, uh, not sure if that would be a good idea." At the wounded expression she gave him, he rushed to explain. "It's just that she's fragile right now. She's on some pretty heavy medication and in a lot of pain. I wouldn't want anything…upsetting her."

"I understand," she said, but it was evident that he'd hurt her feelings.

"Jane—"

"I'm curious about something," she said. "Why do you cut your mom's lawn?"

As always, her rapid shift of subject threw him. "Well, she's had back problems for years. It's too strenuous for her."

"But, why do *you* have to do it?"

"You heard Lisa. She does everything else."

A tiny wrinkle of frustration formed in her brow. "I guess what I'm asking is, if money isn't an issue, and you're pressed for time, why not hire a lawn service?"

"Ugh." He collapsed back on the table, throwing an arm over his face. "We're going to have one of *those* discussions, aren't we? The kind where I walk away feeling like a heel."

"I don't mean to make you feel like a heel. Honestly. I'm just trying to understand why you feel it's your responsibility."

"Look, I know you don't understand this, but since my father died I feel responsible for my mom and Lisa. They've been very dependent on me. If I don't keep on top of things, I feel as if I'm failing him somehow."

"Have you ever considered that they're perfectly capable of taking care of themselves. Don't you owe that to them? I mean, what were to happen if, God forbid, you were injured in the line of duty. What if you were killed? What would they do then?"

He didn't answer. He only lifted his arm and gave her that look, the one that said she was butting her nose in where it didn't belong. She knew she was pushing her luck, yet for reasons she didn't understand, she couldn't seem to let it drop. "Is there a day that Lisa doesn't call you for something?"

He snorted. "I wish."

"Wouldn't it be nice if she didn't?"

He gave her a *duh* look.

"Then why not hire her some help? Have someone come in a couple hours a week to stay with your mom so Lisa gets a break. If you take some of the pressure off her, maybe she'll lighten up on you."

"I could never entrust my mother to a stranger. She would hate that."

"Have you ever asked her?"

"Jane—"

She held up a hand. "I know, I know—butt out."

"I should probably finish this so we can get out of here." Mitch sat up and hopped down from the table, signifying the end of the discussion.

At least he was talking to her again. And little did he know, it was far from over. Just delayed. "I guess I'll go back inside."

As she started across the lawn, the mower sputtered back to life. She heard a loud *thunk,* then a shaft of pain pierced the back of her head, throwing her forward. She felt herself falling in slow motion, until she hit the ground hard on her knees. Stunned, she curled into a ball, cradling her head. She could smell the earth and feel the cool grass against her forehead, but everything felt fuzzy and surreal.

Get up!

She heard the harsh voice vibrate through her mind. *Answer me, or I'll make you sorry.*

An unexpected wave of terror gripped her, stealing her breath. It rose up from somewhere deep inside, paralyzing her. She wasn't even sure what she was afraid of, she only knew that she had to run, to hide. He was looking for her, lurking in the shadows. A nameless, faceless presence so sinister, so evil, it was barely human.

Run, a voice inside of her pleaded, but she couldn't move. She couldn't think past the numbing fear. Then she felt pressure on the back of her head, the warmth of a hand on her back.

He was going to get her. *Punish* her.

"*Jane. Look at me.*"

Her eyes shot open at the impassioned plea, focused on the face gazing down at her. The gentle brown eyes filled with concern.

The surge of relief she felt left her weak and trembling.

"Christ, you scared me," Mitch said, his own voice thick with relief. "When you wouldn't answer me, I had this fear that you would wake up and not know who you were and we would have to start all over again."

"What happened?"

"Something shot out from under the mower and hit you in the head. You're bleeding." He held his bloodstained T-shirt for her to see. She winced when he reapplied it to her stitches. It hurt, but nothing like the pain when she'd awoken in the hospital.

"Are you okay? Can you stand?"

"I think so." She took his hand and he helped pull her

to her feet, but a wave of dizziness buckled her knees from under her.

"Whoa." Mitch caught her under one arm. "Maybe you should sit down for a minute."

"Good idea." She leaned into him as he led her to the picnic table and sat next to her. She let her head fall to his shoulder, sighed as he stroked the hair back from her face. The crippling fear had eased. She felt safe now—but for how long? He was still out there. She didn't even know who he was, yet she could feel him waiting, biding his time. "Something has changed."

He brushed his knuckles across her cheek, down the line of her jaw. "What do you mean?"

"Someone is after me. Someone…evil. And I don't think it's the man from the store. This is different." She lifted her head, looking up at him. His eyes were narrowed, his brow creased with concern. "It's so close. I can feel something happening. I can't even explain it. I only know that something has changed."

"You're remembering," he said. "It's coming back to you. I could see it when you looked up at me. You expected to see someone else, didn't you?"

Biting her lip, she nodded. "I can't see his face, I can't hear his voice, but I know he's there. And there was something else, something I couldn't quite put my finger on, but now I think I understand."

"What?"

"Not only was I terrified, but I felt so…alone. Like there wasn't anyone to help me. Anyone who cared. I felt hollowed-out and empty."

The arm around her tightened. "You're not alone. I'm with you until we figure this out. I promise."

With a swell of gratitude and warmth also came the realization that she trusted him implicitly. And though every instinct warned her against it, it was almost a relief. As if some burden had been lifted.

Without thinking, she reached up to touch his face, smoothed the crease in the corner of one eye with her thumb. He covered her hand with his own, pressing it to his cheek. Then the back door flew open, crashing against the aluminum siding, and they both turned in the direction of the commotion.

Lisa charged out toward them. "What happened? I saw you go down but I was helping mom to the bathroom and I couldn't leave her. Are you hurt?"

"Something flew out from under the lawnmower and pegged me in the head," Jane said. "I'm all right now."

"Are you bleeding?" Lisa brushed her brother's hand away and lifted the compress. "Eww. Does it hurt?"

"A little."

Lisa pressed the shirt firmly to her head.

"Lisa, what on earth is happening out there?" The demand originated from the back of the house and Jane turned to search out the source—a shadow behind the screen of the bedroom window. Mitch's mother.

Uh-oh.

"Christ," Lisa muttered, rolling her eyes heavenward. "The doctor keeps telling her not to get up by herself. Does she ever listen?"

"Nothing is happening, Mom," Mitch shouted across

the yard to the open window. "Go back to bed. Everything is fine." He turned to his sister and hissed under his breath, "Get in there and make her lie down before she hurts herself."

Lisa curled her hands into tight fists, hissing back, "Why don't *you* go in and make her do it. I'm sick of fighting her."

"Who is that out there with you, Mitch?" their mother called.

"No one," Mitch called back, looking nervously to Jane, as if he thought she might spontaneously shout out her identity.

"Oh! Is that the amnesia woman Lisa told me about?"

Mitch shot Lisa a look of pure venom. "You *told* her."

Lisa shrugged, like she didn't see the big deal. "Sorry. Jeez, I didn't know it was a secret."

"Bring her inside, I'd like to meet her," their mother ordered, her shadow fading from the window.

"Aw, hell, now where does she think she's going?" Mitch dashed toward the house, Lisa close behind. Jane followed, holding the shirt to her head. By the time they all piled through the back door, Mitch's mother was clearing the kitchen doorway.

Jane hovered behind Mitch, struggling to reconcile the image of the frail, fragile woman she'd pictured, with the vibrant, alert woman standing across the room. Mrs. Thompson stood only a few inches shorter than her son, was slim and athletic, and though she clutched the wall for support, the pain of her efforts stark on her face, she was anything but frail. Even in her physically compromised condition she had an air of sturdiness about her, a stance that said, "Just try and mess with me."

Jane liked her instantly.

"What has the doctor said about you getting out of bed by yourself?" Lisa scolded, speaking to her mother as if she were a naughty child.

Her mother waved it off. "Mitch honey, help me to the couch."

With a backward glance at Jane—one that said, "make yourself invisible"—Mitch slid an arm around his mother's waist and led her into the living room. "Shouldn't you be lying down? I can take you back to your room."

"Do you need a pain pill?" Lisa asked. "It's been over four hours since your last one."

"The way you two go on you'd think I had my brain removed." With Mitch's assistance, she lowered herself gingerly onto the couch. "If I didn't think I could get up by myself, I wouldn't try, and if I need a damned pain pill I'll ask for one."

This little domestic scene was touching, and Jane couldn't have felt more out of place. She didn't belong here. Mitch had made that more than clear. As quietly as possible she edged backward to the door, thinking she could make a stealthy escape. She was reaching for the door handle when Mrs. Thompson said sternly, "Where do you think you're going?"

Busted. Jane cringed, hitching a thumb over her shoulder. "Um…outside?"

"Oh, no you're not. I've never met anyone with amnesia before. Mitch, introduce me to your friend."

"Mom, she's not my—"

She stopped him mid-sentence with a look that could curdle milk. "She has a name, doesn't she?"

"We're using the name Jane," he said.

Jane approached her with an outstretched hand, wondering if she might get it bitten off in the process. "It's nice to meet you, Mrs. Thompson."

Mitch's mom took her hand and held it. "What happened to your head, dear?"

Jane realized that she was still pressing the shirt to her stitches and pulled it away. "Something flew out from under the mower. I think it split my stitches."

"We should probably take you to the hospital and have that looked at," Mitch said, looking desperate to leave. "I'll get my keys."

Mrs. Thompson ignored him and tugged on Jane's arm. "Sit. Let me take a look at that."

"It's fine, really."

Her grip on Jane's hand increased, to the point of pain. "*Sit.*"

O-o-okay. Jane sat, wondering if Mitch's mom had ever been a drill sergeant.

"Don't worry, I'm a nurse." She parted the hair gently and inspected Jane's stitches. "The stitches are intact. It stopped bleeding but the area is inflamed. Lisa, get me a cold compress and a bottle of ibuprofen. That should take down the swelling." She turned to Mitch. "She's staying with you?"

Mitch nodded, head bowed, looking repentant. It suddenly dawned on Jane why he hadn't wanted her around his mother. She'd been a cop's wife. As such, she knew darned well he shouldn't be letting Jane stay at his house. He didn't want her to know, because he didn't want her mad at him—or even worse, disappointed. Not that Jane could blame him. Mitch's mom didn't seem the type to take disappointment well.

"He's been respectful?" Mrs. Thompson asked her.

She glanced up and saw Mitch's eyes widen a fraction. What? Did he honestly think she would rat him out? Besides, when he'd cornered her in the kitchen that morning, and plastered her to the door in the stairwell that afternoon, she'd never once felt that he'd compromised her principles. He'd ravished her with the utmost respect.

"Very respectful," Jane said finally.

"Your lieutenant knows?" Mitch's mother asked him. Mitch gave her a single nod.

"You're in good hands, dear." She smiled and patted Jane's hand, then turned to Mitch. "Go finish the grass, I'll entertain our guest while Lisa makes lunch. And Lisa, get your brother a clean shirt to wear home. Oh, and throw this one in the wash before the blood sets."

Lisa handed over the compress and a bottle of ibuprofen, then snatched the shirt from her mother's hand and stomped away, mumbling under her breath.

"You, out," Mitch's mother told him, pointing to the back door.

"Mom—"

"Shoo!" She waved him away. "Out of here. We'll have a nice chat, won't we, Jane?"

Her tone was pleasant, her smile genuine, yet the hair on the back of Jane's neck prickled with apprehension.

Oh, boy, what had she gotten herself into this time? She turned to Mitch, with an expression that she hoped screamed, *help me!*

He just grinned and disappeared out the door.

"Fragile?" Jane asked from the passenger's side of the car. "You think your mother is *fragile?"*

He swallowed back a grin. "What I meant was, she's heavily medicated. She's not herself."

"She's…tough."

"She was a cop's wife. She had to be tough."

"And she's unbelievably proud of you. But she wants to see you settle down. And she *really* wants grandchildren."

"I know," he grumbled. He'd been hearing that one for years.

"But she says you're afraid of commitment."

Mitch cringed. Way to go Mom. "Oh, yeah? And how exactly would she know that?"

"Because you never date women long enough to bring them home to meet her."

"You guys had a nice talk, huh?"

"She kept asking me about my family and where I went to school. I had to remind her about twenty times that I don't remember anything."

"Sorry about that. It's probably the medication." He pulled into his driveway, threw the car into Park and shut off the engine. "The truth is, she's always been a bit left of center."

"I liked her."

"She has her moments."

"Your sister looked pretty mad when we left." She tugged on the sleeve of the shirt Lisa had given him. "You think she's trying to tell you something?"

He glanced down at the phrase across his chest: I Used To Have A Handle On Life, But It Broke. "I don't doubt that she was."

"I like Lisa, and your mom. If things were different…"

"They're not."

She bit her lip, a wounded look on her face, and he felt like a jerk for hurting her feelings yet again. But he couldn't let her get attached.

Hell, who was he kidding? He couldn't let *himself* get attached. It felt too damned good having Jane around. Like coming home after being away for a really long time. It didn't help that both his mom and Lisa had taken to her immediately. And as quirky as those two could be, they were both excellent judges of character.

As if that made a difference.

"I didn't mean to imply that I hoped things *were* different," she said. She sounded so lost. Dejected. "I know they can't be. I just think it would be nice to get to know your family better. Your mom is funny and smart." She gazed out the windshield, her eyes misting over. "I've missed having a mother."

"She passed away?" he asked before he realized what he was saying, that she didn't know who her mother even was. It was just a natural question to her statement. He couldn't believe it when she actually answered him.

"I don't see her anymore," she said, her voice sounding distant and sad.

She was remembering. She didn't even realize it, but

she was telling him about her past. She looked almost entranced, completely lost in thought.

"Why don't you see her, Jane?"

She looked up at him, the fog that settled over her eyes clearing, "See who?"

"Your mother. You said you don't see her anymore."

She frowned. "When did I say that?"

"Just now. You said you missed your mother. I asked if she died and you said you don't see her anymore. When I asked why, you snapped out of it." He swore and smacked his forehead. "I called you Jane."

She pressed a hand to her heart, eyes lighting with excitement. "I'm remembering things, aren't I?"

"I think so."

"Just like you said. When I stopped trying, it came to me." The smile slipped from her face. "Uh-oh."

"What's wrong?"

She nodded toward his window. "Arnold's back."

Mitch swiveled in his seat. Darren stood on the driveway just outside Mitch's door, and he didn't look happy. Mitch's first instinct was to laugh because Jane was right; Darren did look like a golf pro. He rolled down his window. "What's up?"

Darren looked from Mitch to Jane then back again. "I was about to ask you the same thing."

What was with everyone lately? Was it bust-Mitch's-chops week? "We just came back from my mother's house," Mitch said. "You checking up on me?"

"I heard about Robby Barrett. I came by to see if you were okay."

"I'm okay."

Again Darren looked suspiciously at Jane, then back again. "You got a minute?"

"Sure." Like he had a choice. No matter what he said or did, Darren would draw his own conclusion and believe whatever it was he wanted to believe. May as well get it over with.

Mitch turned to Jane and said in a low voice, "I'm sorry about this."

She gave him an understanding smile that warmed him to his bones and wracked him with guilt. She didn't deserve Darren's antipathy. Didn't deserve it and certainly didn't need it, yet she took it in stride.

"It's okay," she said quietly. "He's your friend. He's worried about you."

They climbed out of the car, and Darren followed them to the porch. The front windows had been replaced while they were gone and the broken glass hauled away. The only evidence of last night's disturbance was the trampled shrubbery and the shredded curtains still dangling in the bedroom window.

Mitch unlocked the door and they all stepped inside. For a moment everyone stood in the foyer, silent. The tension was so thick, it was like wading through wet sand.

"I need to speak to you," Darren said, glancing meaningfully in Jane's direction. *"Alone."*

"If you'll both excuse me," Jane said, backing toward the hall.

Mitch started toward her. "Jane—"

"Nope, it's okay. I'm going to take a shower. You two have a nice little chat."

Mitch watched as she scurried down the hall, then he

heard the bathroom door shut. She knew as well as he did, a nice little chat was the last thing he and Darren would be having.

"So?" Darren said. "Having fun, Mitch?"

Chapter 12

Mitch turned to Darren. "Having fun doing what?"

"Playing house." Darren leaned casually against the wall, hands in his pants pockets, cocky as hell. But that was typical for him. "That is what you're doing, right?"

"I'm not even going to justify that with a response."

Darren speared him with an accusing glare. "Why can't you see what's so obvious to everyone else? You're losing your objectivity. After Kim, I thought you would be smarter than this."

That one stung. And though Mitch hated to admit it, Darren was right. What grip Mitch did have on his emotions was slipping away. When Jane had been hit in the head earlier, when he called her name and she wouldn't answer, he'd been scared half out of his wits and teetering on the edge of total panic. In his line of work, that was unacceptable. It meant he'd lost his ability to reason, to look at Jane's situation objectively, and that was a very bad thing. Not to mention dangerous.

Mitch collapsed on the couch, throwing his head back against the cushions and shutting his eyes. Now, if he could just shut out his best friend's words, or his own doubts.

"You look like you could use a beer," Darren said.

It would take more than a beer to fix this mess, to numb the attraction he felt for Jane, but it couldn't hurt. Without opening his eyes he answered, "Sure, I'll take a beer."

He heard Darren walk to the kitchen, heard the fridge open, the clink of glass bottles. He could also hear the shower in the next room through the wall, and couldn't stop himself from imagining Jane in there. Or imagining himself joining her under the spray, soaping every inch of that satiny soft skin.

"You're sleeping with her."

Mitch opened his eyes, looked up at Darren. "Is that a question?"

He handed Mitch one of the two beers he was holding. "I don't know, is it?"

"If I tell you I'm not, will you believe me?"

"No." Darren sat on the love seat across from him. He leaned forward, resting his elbows on his knees, taking a long pull on his beer, then another. "I don't know. Maybe."

Mitch raised the bottle to his lips, took a swallow, but the cool brew tasted bitter to his overwrought senses. Compared to the sweetness of Jane's kiss. It was that sweetness he was craving now, like an addict craves his next fix. It was more intoxicating than any liquor he'd ever consumed and as addictive as any drug.

He set the beer down on the end table, but it slipped from his grip. Before he could right it, it toppled over and the majority of its contents sloshed onto the rug. "Damn it!"

"I'll get something to clean it up." Darren dashed from the room and returned several seconds later with a roll of paper towels. He tore off a handful and dropped them on the stain, then used his foot to absorb the spill. "You are in bad shape, aren't you?"

"I'm not sleeping with her," Mitch said.

Darren wadded up the wet paper towels and tossed them onto the glass-top coffee table. "Why do I sense a 'yet' missing from that statement?"

"Because you're a cynic." Mitch leaned forward, cursing. He rubbed the heels of his palms into his eyes. "Because you know me too well."

"What if she's married. What if she's into something illegal. Another fiasco like Kim and they won't let it slide. They'll have your badge this time."

"You think I don't know that?"

"To make matters worse, you've got a dead rapist and a family out for blood. That doesn't look real good, either. They're convinced he was innocent."

"Do you think he was guilty?"

"Yeah, I think he was guilty. Did you have any proof to the contrary?"

"It doesn't work that way. The burden of proof falls on us. And after interrogating the guy for twelve hours,

I can't honestly say he was capable of committing those rapes. He had the mental capacity of a twelve-year-old."

Darren snorted. "And the rap sheet of a career criminal."

"I'm not denying the guy was a sexual deviant, but indecent exposure is a hell of a stretch from brutal rape. And why did he only have one of the two items taken from each victim? How did he manage to leave behind not a shred of physical evidence. It doesn't add up."

"What are you suggesting?"

"I think he was set up. I think whoever committed those rapes planted the evidence in his apartment. They knew Robby lived alone and usually went out at night to local bars. They knew he had a record. I think the real rapist followed him and chose his victims in places Robby had been."

"So what do you plan to do? If you're right about this, how do you find the real rapist? If it hadn't been for the anonymous tip, we'd still be scratching our heads over this one. There's no evidence. Not to mention that the case is closed."

"I'm not sure what I'm going to do."

"I'll tell you exactly what you should do. Until you can prove otherwise keep your mouth shut. If your theory gets back to the family you're screwed." Darren pulled himself up from the couch and set his half-empty bottle down next to Mitch's. "You don't want to be responsible for a lawsuit that could potentially cost the city millions in damages."

Yeah, that would go over real well with the department. After they were through with him, he would be lucky to get a job working security at the mall.

"This thing with your new girlfriend. Maybe she is the genuine article. That doesn't mean that when she gets her memory back, and she's reunited with her family, she isn't going to drop you flat. Either way, you lose. And if she is mixed up in something illegal, or on the run, I don't have to tell you what a mess that would be."

Mitch leaned back and closed his eyes again. Though he'd prefer not to hear the words coming from Darren, it was nothing he hadn't already considered. At this point, he might not have a choice. He was already in too deep.

He heard Darren walk across the room and let himself out, the new panes of glass rattling in their frame as he shut the door hard behind him.

"Tough to argue with logic like that."

Mitch opened his eyes. Jane stood in the living room doorway, watching him. Damp hair hung to her shoulders and was brushed back, making her eyes look wide and innocent. Nearly childlike. Which only kicked up his level of guilt. She wore Lisa's old robe, belted loosely at the waist. He couldn't stop himself from wondering if she wore anything underneath, or remembering the way her hips curved perfectly into his palms, the swell of her breast cupped in his hand. The way they'd fit together just right as they lay on the bedroom floor.

He shook away the memory. "Who says logic has anything to do with this. When every instinct I have tells me we're headed for disaster, and I still can't keep my hands off of you. That's not logical."

Jane crossed the room and stood before him, wondering what would happen if she jumped down from the wall. Would he catch her? And even if he did, would it be the smart thing to do? She knew without question, despite the amnesia, she'd never wanted a man the way she wanted Mitch. This connection, this soul-wrenching gut-level need to be close to another human being couldn't possibly happen more than once in a lifetime. And maybe it wasn't smart, maybe it was downright foolish, but it was what they both *needed*. The consequences be damned.

"What we feel for each other now isn't going to change when I get my memory back," she said.

He looked up at her, eyes filled with some unreadable expression. If she didn't know better, she would say he looked vulnerable. "You don't know that."

That's when she realized, this had a hell of a lot more to do with his fear of commitment than any conflict of interest. He was scared. He didn't want his heart broken.

Well, she was scared, too. She had just as much to lose.

To hell with jumping down, this was one wall she intended to knock over permanently.

Mitch leaned forward and grasped the ties on her robe, pulling her closer. He pressed his forehead to her stomach, wrapped his hands over her hips, digging his fingers into her flesh. Her head got that thick, swimmy feeling and heat pooled between her thighs.

"I shouldn't be touching you like this," he growled, his fingers curling into the flannel. She gasped as the fabric rode higher up her thighs. "If you were smart you would walk away."

"I'm not going anywhere." Instead, Jane climbed into his lap, straddling his legs, but when she tried to touch him, he grasped her wrists.

"Tell me you don't need this as much as I do," she said.

For a minute he only looked at her, then he cursed and dropped his hands to his sides. "What we're doing is completely nuts."

"Maybe, but completely nuts seems to be working for us. Why spoil a good thing?"

He reached up to cradle her face in his palms, brushed his mouth over hers, and everything in the world felt right again. She savored the gentle pressure of his lips, so tender and sweet. And, oh, did he know how to kiss. She felt herself sinking deeper under his spell, longing building low in her belly. She inhaled the scent of his hair, his skin. He smelled of sun and shampoo and freshly cut grass.

She threaded her fingers through his hair and he moaned. He held her closer, kissed deeper. Her pulse pounded hard and fast. She ached for him to fill the hollow place inside of her, to make her feel whole again.

He pulled the robe off her shoulder, kissed her there, nipping with his teeth. She grasped the hem of his shirt, lifted it up over his head, taking in the sight of all that tanned skin, taut over lean muscle. Tentatively she reached out to touch him, watching her own hands as she smoothed her palms down his chest, over the sparse hair circling his small dark nipples.

"Damn," he breathed. "Nothing that feels this good should be legal."

She gasped as his hands settled over her hips firmly, possessively, pulling her intimately against him. It frightened and excited her all at once. Boldly, she let her hands drift lower. The muscles of his stomach coiled under her touch, and his grip on her tightened. She wanted more—every part of her throbbed to feel his touch—but when he reached for the tie on her robe, tugged it loose, uncertainty sent her hands flying up to stop him.

"Don't tell me you're going shy on me now," he said.

She wasn't sure what was wrong with her, where this sudden doubt was coming from. "I—I don't know why I did that."

He curled his fingers through hers. "Someone hurt you."

"Maybe." She watched with fascination as he raised her hands to his lips, kissing her fingers, one by one.

"I'm not going to hurt you." He kissed her temple, her cheek, the corner of her mouth. She never imagined that he could be so tender and gentle. She let her head roll back, closing her eyes as he kissed the column of her throat, her collarbone, between her breasts. With every brush of his lips, each whisper of his breath against her skin, her apprehension dissolved a little bit more.

He nudged the robe aside, exposing the very tops of her breasts, tracing the slight swell with his thumbs. As the robe slid off her shoulders, down her arms, she smothered the urge to reach up and cover herself.

Mitch gently cupped her breasts in his palms. He caressed with his thumbs, each pass making her quiver, making the blood surge faster through her veins. This time she didn't try to stop him when he pulled the ties loose on her robe. She held her breath as it slipped to the floor, leaving her completely exposed. Though instinct told her she should be feeling vulnerable and reserved, the look in Mitch's eyes—the unguarded appreciation—showed her he was risking just as much. He was exposing himself emotionally.

It made her want him even more.

"You're so beautiful," he said, running his hands over her skin, his touch barely more than a tease. With trembling fingers, she unhooked his belt and unfastened his jeans, rising up on her knees, so he could pull them down. Instead, he hooked an arm around her waist, hauled her against his chest and slipped a hand between her thighs.

That first touch, the first stroke of his fingers, rocked through her like pure energy. She gasped, gripping his shoulders.

He stroked lightly, focusing on the center of her heat. The place that burned for his touch. His eyes locked on her face. There was an intensity there, a hunger that frightened and thrilled her. Her legs felt weak and her head dizzy. She knew deep in her soul that no other man had ever made her feel this way. A feeling this exquisite, so purely physical yet deeply emotional, would be impossible to forget.

He stopped long enough to shove his jeans and boxers down and kick them away, then he pulled her back down into his lap. He sank his fingers into her hair, locked his mouth over hers. The kiss was deep and searching—desperate. It never ceased to amaze her how much of himself he put into every kiss, every touch.

She arched against him, searching him out, and gasped at the sheer intimacy of their position, at her need to feel him inside of her. Before the hollow place swallowed her up and she ceased to exist.

"My wallet," he groaned against her mouth, his voice raspy. "I need my wallet."

Reaching back, she groped for his pants and scooped them up off the floor. He wrenched his wallet free and pulled out a condom. She watched with utter fascination as he tore the package open with his teeth and rolled it on. He was so beautiful, so perfect.

He scooped her out of his lap and laid her on the couch cushions, lowering himself over her, and she felt a brief, yet undeniable flash of panic.

Mitch froze. "Something's wrong."

"No. It's just, for a second I felt…trapped."

Mitch held himself very still above her. "Do you trust me?"

That he'd cared enough to ask spoke volumes about the kind of man he was. Emotion clogged her throat, stealing her voice. If she tried to speak she would only burst into tears. So to show him just how deeply that trust ran, she wove her arms around his neck, wrapped her legs over his hips, and eased him into the cradle of her thighs. In one slow smooth thrust he sank down, filled her, his weight pressing her deeper into the cushions. There was no fear, no apprehension, only sweet fulfillment. With every carefully measured thrust, he drove her closer to satisfaction, until the world became a blur of scents and sounds and sensation.

Her last coherent thought before she gave into bliss was that Mitch had been right. This felt too good. Too perfect. Then she stopped thinking altogether.

* * *

Cold. She felt so cold and alone. The edges of her vision were blurred and dark and no matter how hard she concentrated she couldn't see clearly. She needed to see, to get out of there, before something bad happened.

She heard a soft whimper and looked down to find a baby cradled in her arms. She squinted, tried to see if it was a boy or a girl. It was hers, yet it wasn't hers.

Then she heard the laugh. It was taunting, evil. She spun around, fear gripping her as she strained to find the source, to see through the fog. The sound seemed to come from everywhere—and nowhere.

It was him. He'd found her again. And she knew what he wanted.

"You can't have my baby," she screamed into the darkness and was answered with another maniacal laugh. She cradled the baby close to her chest, but her arms were suddenly empty. "No!"

Then she saw him, a shadowy figure drifting just outside of her vision. He wasn't going to take the baby from her. Not this time. She tried to run toward him but her legs felt weighted down. She forced them to move, pushing with all her strength, picking up speed, yet every time she felt she was getting closer, he disappeared around a corner.

All around her faceless people watched, but did nothing. No one would help her. Then she saw them. Her parents. She couldn't see their faces, but she knew it was them.

"He took my baby. Stop him," she pleaded.

"So spoiled," they said sadly. "Never happy with what you have. Always breaking our hearts."

"Please, help me," she begged, but when she reached for them, they faded away.

Then she felt hands gripping her arms. It was him. She had to fight, she had to get free!

"Jane!"

Her eyes flew open. She was struggling, pushing up against the hands restraining her. Then she saw that it was Mitch looking down at her through the dark. She looked around, realized she was in his bedroom, in his bed.

"Easy," he said, his voice low and soothing.

Her body went slack against the mattress. She was with Mitch. She was safe.

He let go of her arms and she threw them around his neck.

He held her close, stroking her hair. "It's okay. It's just a dream."

"I remember it this time. There was a man chasing me." A shudder raced up her spine. "I was holding a baby and he took it."

"Who was he?"

"I don't know, but my parents were there, too, and they wouldn't help me."

"You saw them?"

"Not their faces, but I knew it was them. I felt so alone."

His arms tightened around her. "You're not alone."

She pressed her cheek against his chest, heard the

steady thump of his heart. His skin was soft and warm and scented with the soap they'd used in the shower earlier that evening.

"It was so strange. It was my baby, but it wasn't. Now I know I don't have kids. I also know this man from my dream is after me. I could... *feel* him. He won't stop until he finds me."

"Whoever he is, I'm not going to let him get you."

"What's going to happen tomorrow when you go in to see your lieutenant?"

"Let me worry about that, okay?" God knows he was doing enough worrying for the both of them. Worrying what would happen when he was inevitably pulled from the case. He was beginning to think it would be for the best. He was getting too attached, and there wasn't a damned thing he could do to stop it. As long as they could find someone they trusted to watch over her. If that person even existed.

He stroked her back and neck, ran his fingers through her hair. Finally she relaxed against him. Her breath was less ragged now, and warm against his neck. Then he felt her mouth against his skin and—*ouch!* She was *biting* him.

"Hey," he said, "didn't we determine the biting is unnecessary?"

She nipped his shoulder and whispered, "What if I promise not to draw blood this time?"

Her hands slid up into his hair and she tangled her fingers through it, pulling his head back so she could reach his throat. Her teeth scraped his Adam's apple, his chin.

"We should get some sleep," he said gruffly.

"I don't want to sleep. Make love to me again."

She kissed him, drawing his lower lip between her teeth. Well, hell, when she put it that way it was hard to say no. He rolled onto his back, reaching for the box of protection on the night table. He barely had time to roll one on before she was on top of him.

Each time they'd made love, she'd gradually dropped her inhibitions, become bolder. He had the sneaking suspicion he'd unleashed some sort of animal.

In the back of his mind he knew he had to put an end to this. He had to be the rational one. It was clear what he had to do.

Tomorrow, he thought, as she sank down, surrounding him in her heat. He would be rational tomorrow.

Nothing was going as planned. Frustration choked him.

Luck. That's all it was. They were very lucky. He could have taken her today. He was so close. But taking her would have meant innocent victims.

He stood in the shadows, watching the house. The lights had gone out hours ago. He knew what they were doing in there. Women knew just what to do to get their way. They used men, treated them like brainless animals. If he could, he would make them all pay.

The pager on his belt vibrated and he checked the display, a smile curling his lips. It was the sign he'd been waiting for. Funny how, in an instant, everything could fall into place. How, after all the searching, the hiding, she'd come running back to him on her own. Proving once and for all, she was the weak one.

It's time, Jane Doe. You've served your purpose.
    *He was ready to begin the final phase. If everything
went as planned, by tomorrow, this would all be over.*

Chapter 13

Jane sat next to Mitch in the car, wringing her hands in the skirt of her dress. He reached over and took her hand, squeezing her fingers. Despite the balmy temperature her fingers were ice cold. "Relax."

She gave him a wobbly smile. "I'm trying. I just have this feeling that something really bad is going to happen today."

"It's nothing I can't handle." He pulled his hand free and put it back on the steering wheel. If he didn't stop touching her he would do something drastic, like turn the car around, take her back home and spend the day making love to her. Then he would miss the meeting with his lieutenant, and something bad *would* happen— he would lose his job.

He just couldn't satisfy the need to be close to her.

It had occurred to him that morning, as he dressed for work, that he should be feeling regret, or at the very least guilt, for what they had done. Sex with a victim was wrong in more ways than he could count. But what they'd experienced last night went so far beyond sex it was difficult to determine exactly what had happened. He'd never connected to a woman like he had with Jane. Not just physically or emotionally, but spiritually. Like two lost souls finding each other and uniting.

Souls uniting? Christ, where was he getting this crap? If Darren heard him talk this way he'd have Mitch committed.

"It's getting closer," Jane said. "I can feel it."

"What's getting closer?"

"My memory. I feel like I'm standing on the edge of a precipice. Someone or something is nudging me from behind, but I'm afraid of what I'm going to find down there. It's so dark and cold. I find myself fighting it, trying not to remember. And the more I fight it the closer it comes." She turned to Mitch, her eyes wide and full of apprehension. "What if it's something really bad."

He tugged on the sleeve of her jacket, coaxing her closer, because he couldn't stand to see her afraid and not do something to soothe her. She slid across the seat, leaning into him, and he tucked an arm around her shoulders. "We'll deal with it, Jane. You're not in this alone."

"The thing is, I don't want you to protect me. I know it probably won't make any sense to you—it doesn't even make sense to me—but I feel like I need to face this alone. Like I should be taking care of myself."

He didn't want her to tackle this alone. He wanted to be there for her. To take care of her. But he knew she would never let him. She would only let him so close. And that hurt more than he wanted to admit. But it made what he had to do a little bit easier. "You're right, that doesn't make sense."

"I know." She blew out a long, frustrated breath, letting her head fall back against the seat.

As they drew closer to the police station, Mitch slowed the car. He couldn't exactly pull into the lot with them sitting this way. "Uh, Jane?"

She looked up at him questioningly.

He nodded to the other side of the bench. "You should probably scoot over."

She looked at the seat, then up at the patrol cars and officers in the station lot. "To give the illusion that we didn't spend the night in bed together?"

"Something like that."

"Gotcha." She slid out of his arms, to the other end of the seat.

He pulled into the lot and parked near the back, steeling himself for what was sure to be a major reaming from his lieutenant.

"If I forget to mention it, it was great," Jane said.

Mitch pulled the keys from the ignition and turned to her. "What was great?"

"Last night. It was…" She sighed, looking wistful. "I would say it was amazing, but it was more than that. It was…all-encompassing. Gigantic."

He lifted a brow at her. "It was *gigantic?*"

She rolled her eyes at him. "God, you are such a

man. I didn't mean *that* was gigantic. Not that it was in-
adequate by any means, but…you're making fun of me."

Dappled sunlight pouring through the windshield
danced against the gold highlights of her hair, making
it shimmer. He longed to reach out and slip his fingers
through it. The need to touch her, to be close to her, was
overwhelming. Her honesty got him every time.

Man, he was in *big* trouble. If he didn't cut her loose
now, he knew he would be sorry.

Jane sat in the squad room, her eye on the door Mitch
had disappeared through nearly twenty minutes earlier.
A shiver of fear trickled along her spine. Here she was
surrounded by police, in quite possibly the safest building in all of Twin Oaks and she couldn't shake a feeling of wariness. She folded her arms around herself,
sinking down in the chair, wishing herself invisible.
Would she never feel safe again?

Across the room, the door swung open and Mitch
emerged followed by Arnold Palmer and another detective she didn't recognize. She bolted up in the chair, trying to read his expression, to guess what may have
transpired. His face was stoic as they crossed to his
desk, and he wouldn't meet her eye.

"Jane," he said, gesturing to the third detective. "This
is Detective Petroski, and you already know Detective
Waite."

Jane looked up at Mitch as if to ask, "What does this
mean to me?" although she already had a pretty good
idea what was coming next.

"As of this morning they've been assigned to your

case. You'll be kept in protective custody until we've either caught the man who attacked you, or feel he no longer poses a threat."

Jane swayed in her seat. Though he didn't come right out and say it, it was clear what had happened. She'd been sure he would catch some heat from his lieutenant, but she never expected him to be yanked from the case.

"I thought we didn't know who we could trust."

"You can trust them."

No, she couldn't. Mitch was the only one she trusted. Didn't he see that? "Don't I have any say in this?"

"No. You don't."

She was about to protest, but something in Mitch's eyes warned her to keep quiet, that by voicing her very strong opinion, she would only make matters worse.

She drew herself up, straightening her spine with as much dignity as she could gather. "All right."

"Detective Petroski is going to take you to a safe house. I'll take you back to my place first so you can pick up your things."

"I'm gonna make the arrangements," Detective Petroski said, looking from Jane to Mitch. "How 'bout we meet back here in about an hour."

Mitch nodded and hooked a hand under Jane's elbow, silently leading her toward the door. She was aware of more than a few pairs of eyes following them as they pushed through the door into the parking lot. He headed for the sedan, unlocked her side and helped her in, then walked around and climbed in behind the wheel.

"I guess it didn't go so well in there," she said.

Mitch stared straight ahead. "It could have been worse."

So selfish, a voice in her head taunted. *Never happy with what you have.*

Was it true? Was this really all her fault?

"I'm so sorry about everything," she said.

He looked over at her, eyes stony. "*Don't* do that. Don't apologize. This isn't your fault. Let's just get your things and get this over with."

Mitch stood in the bedroom doorway, wallowing in his own personal hell, drowning in guilt as he watched Jane stuff her few belongings in the duffel bag he'd given her. He'd never expected to feel this way. This…miserable.

"That's all of it," she said. "Everything I own."

"Let's go." He moved aside, so she could walk past him.

Instead she tossed the bag down and stared at him, arms crossed stubbornly over her chest, jaw set. "Oh, no. You're not getting off that easy. We're going to talk about this."

"There's nothing to talk about," he said, but he could see the determination in her stance, the set of her jaw. She wasn't going to let him off the hook. She wouldn't give an inch.

It was what he admired most about her, and it could be annoying as hell. Particularly at a time like this. Couldn't she see that this was for the best? That getting mixed up with him was a bad idea? That he would hurt her?

"Mitch, don't shut me out now. I want to know what's going to happen. Is this it for us?"

He lowered his eyes to the floor. Christ, he couldn't even look at her. If he did, if he saw hope there—or pain—he would be a goner. They needed to make a clean break. "It would be in both of our best interests if we back off."

"In our *best interests?* Would you stop being a cop for two minutes and talk to me?"

"I am a cop. It's not something I can shut off."

"Can you at least tell me if we'll see each other again?"

"You mean, ever?"

"Yes. *Ever.*"

He finally looked at her, and damn it, he shouldn't have. There was so much pain there, so much hurt. "Maybe it would be better if we didn't."

"So I'm just supposed to forget what happened last night? Pretend it meant nothing?"

"Maybe it did. Maybe it was just sex to me."

Now she was mad. Her eyes went dark with indignation. "You are such a liar. And a coward."

"Yeah, so sue me," he grumbled.

"Go to hell," she said, then she shoved him—actually planted her hands on his chest and pushed so hard he stumbled back. Then she spun around and started out the bedroom door, but not before he saw the tears in her eyes, and that was his undoing.

"Jane, wait." He grabbed her wrist and dragged her back to him.

"Let me go," she said, trying to snatch her arm away, but he pulled her to him anyway. She resisted for about a half a second, then went limp against him.

"I'm sorry," he said. "I didn't mean that. Last night was great. It was *too* great. But you don't want to get mixed up with me. Can't you see that ending this would be in your best interest?"

Her voice was muffled against his shirt. "If I always did what was in my best interest, I probably wouldn't be in this mess in the first place."

"What do you want from me, Jane?"

She looked up at him, her eyes mirroring his own frustration. "I don't want anything—and I want *everything*."

He couldn't stop himself, he had to kiss her one last time. He tilted her head up, pressed his lips to hers. Just one more kiss.

But he knew instantly that a kiss would never be enough, when she tangled her fingers through his hair, pressed her body against him. Arousal slammed him from all sides.

Her eyes dark with desire, Jane reached down and rubbed a hand over the fly of his dress pants. He wanted to do the right thing, but damn it, he couldn't deny he wanted her. For all the wrong reasons. And all the right ones, which was even worse. And if he'd had an ounce of blood left in his brain, a scrap of good sense, he would have pushed her away. But he needed to be inside of her. One more time. Even if she ended up hating him for it.

He unzipped the back of her dress, shoved the straps down and watched it fall to the floor around her feet, exposing every perfect inch of her body. He would never get tired of this, tired of looking at her, touching her. He lowered his head, took one pale pink nipple into his mouth and she gasped, arching against him. He loved making her feel good. He slipped a hand between her thighs, stroked her. She moaned and arched against his hand. She was so wet for him, so ready. He couldn't not make love to her.

She fumbled with his belt and unfastened his pants, yanking them open, then shoved his sport jacket off his shoulders. When she started undoing the buttons on his shirt, he stopped her.

"No time," he said. He backed her against the bedroom wall, then remembered the condom. Definitely couldn't forget that. "Grab my wallet."

She did, and rather than handing him the foil package, she ripped it open and rolled it on for him. He was sure he'd died and gone to heaven on the spot.

And he'd never felt so alive in his life.

He pinned her to the wall, lifting her right off her feet, and she wrapped her legs around his waist. He was almost completely dressed, with a sexy, naked woman in his arms. It was the most erotic thing he'd ever experienced.

In one quick, not-so-gentle thrust, he was deep inside her. Each time their bodies joined he swore it felt a million times better than the last. She clung to him, a bundle of silky skin and slick heat.

"Tell me you want me," she demanded breathlessly. "Tell me you want me as much as I want you."

"I want you," he said and crushed his mouth down on hers. She tasted sweet and dangerous. Dangerous because the L word was insinuating itself into what should be plain old sex. Plain old, mind-blowing, screaming-hot sex.

He couldn't deny it. What they were doing right now, what they'd done last night, was so much more than that.

He tried to pace himself, but he wanted hard and fast and hot and she didn't seem to mind. He felt it the instant she began to climax. She threw back her head and cried out and her body clenched around him. His own release swept over him swift and intense, locking his muscles and stealing his strength. Without the wall to support them, they would have both been on the floor.

"We're getting really good at that," Jane said breathlessly.

He grunted his agreement. If he opened his mouth, he'd wind up saying something he regretted. Something he didn't really mean, like, I love you, or marry me. Amazing sex could do that to a man.

"It hasn't always been like this," she said.

"What do you mean?"

"I get the feeling, there was a time when I didn't have a choice."

Mitch swore under his breath. "I don't know if I want to hear this."

"I'm not talking about rape. More like…duty. I think I did what was expected of me."

He looked her in the eyes, because it was important that she knew he meant what he said. "I didn't plan this and I didn't expect it."

She smiled, smoothing a hand across his cheek. "I know. That's what makes it so special."

And it had to end here. A few more minutes with her this way and he wouldn't be responsible for his actions. "This doesn't change things."

She nodded. "I know."

He gently lowered her to her feet. "We have to get going. They'll be expecting us."

She reached down and grabbed her dress from the carpet. While she dressed, he went into the bathroom and cleaned himself up.

After all they had been through, could he just leave it like this? Shouldn't he at least try to explain?

"I'm ready," she said, appearing in the bathroom doorway. "Let's get this over with."

"It's not you," he said.

"What's not me?"

"Why this won't work. I just don't think it would be a good idea for us to get involved. My life is complicated right now."

"Spare me the it's-not-you-it's-me crap," she said with her usual sass, but underneath it he could hear the hurt in her voice. "If you had genuine feelings for me, we could work things out."

"It's not that simple. I have responsibilities."

"In other words, between work, and Lisa and your mom, where would you fit me in?"

"Something like that."

"Of course it has nothing to do with your fear of commitment." She tucked her bag under her arm. "We have to go. My new baby-sitters will be expecting us."

Mitch followed her to the front door, letting her believe what she wanted to believe. He was doing the right thing, putting an end to this before they got too attached to each other. And she was wrong. This wasn't about any fear of commitment. Like she said, where would he fit her into his life? There was no doubt in his mind she wouldn't settle for second place. She was also fiercely independent, and wouldn't let herself be taken care of. The woman was a walking contradiction. And he had the feeling, when she got her memory back, it would only get more complicated.

He was doing her a favor by ending it now. So why did he feel like such a slime? And if he thought it was for the best, why did he feel so damned sick inside?

When they got to the station, Detective Petroski and Darren met them in the lobby.

Detective Petroski took Jane's bag. "I'll get her set up and take first shift. Darren'll relieve me at ten."

"Swell," Jane mumbled under her breath, barely loud enough for Mitch to hear, and he felt another shot of guilt. Not that it was any consolation, but Darren didn't look too thrilled with the arrangement, either.

"I'll keep you posted from this end," Mitch told them. "The second I get a break, I'll call you."

"It was a tough call," Darren said. "You did the right thing. She'll be safer with us."

Jane narrowed her eyes at Darren. "What was a tough call?"

Knowing what was coming next, Mitch steeled himself. She wouldn't understand, it had been the only thing he could do. The only way to keep her safe.

"Offering to hand the case off to someone else," Darren said.

Mitch had let her believe he'd been removed from the case. Knowing he'd given her up voluntarily, after promising to keep her safe, had to sting. She had to feel betrayed.

Mitch waited for the explosion, for Jane to let him have it.

She didn't bat an eyelash.

"I'm ready to go," she told Petroski, then she turned to Mitch. The look she gave him was so cold he nearly shivered. "So long, Detective."

As they walked through the door, Petroski called back to him. "I'll call you later, let you know when we're settled in."

Jane didn't give him a second glance.

The guilt Mitch had been feeling transformed to an unmistakable sense of unease. He hoped like hell Petroski knew what he was getting himself into, hoped he could handle her.

Jane's silence alone told Mitch, without a doubt, she was up to something.

"Not the talkative type, are you?"

Jane looked over at Detective Petroski, careful to keep the bored expression firmly in place, when in truth, rage was eating her alive inside. "Sue me."

He shrugged. "I'm just trying to be sociable. Don't talk, what do I care?"

Jane sucked in a deep, even breath. Despite his greased-back hair, annoying smoking habit and all-around general ickiness, Detective Petroski didn't deserve to be the target of her anger. He hadn't betrayed her. He hadn't promised—*promised*—they would solve her case together. He didn't swear she wasn't alone, then dump her the first opportunity he got.

Mitch had done that. And the anger, the rage, was the

only thing that kept her functioning. When she let it drop, even for an instant, that crippling pain crept in to take its place.

Apparently, last night had meant nothing to him. He'd slept with her, all the while knowing he was going to dump her in the morning. And this afternoon—he could have told her the truth. He had the opportunity. How could he make love to her knowing he'd betrayed her?

He'd made it quite clear what she had suspected all along. She was in this alone. The only person she could depend on was herself.

Petroski's phone rang, and by the tone of the conversation, she was pretty sure taking this case had gotten him in hot water.

"I told you, Ellen, I gotta work tonight…no, I couldn't get out of it…I know, but—" He swore and closed his phone.

"Ellen is your wife?" Jane asked. Ellen. Why did that name sound so familiar?

"Girlfriend. We were supposed to go out to dinner." *Ellen*. She ran the name over in her head. She *knew* that name. And at the same time, it wasn't right. Was it her? Was it an acquaintance?

Ellen.

She needed a last name to go with it. It was something simple, something easy to remember. She could almost picture it. Ellen Smith. Ellen Jones. Ellen Andrews. Ellen…

Phillips.

Her heart slammed the wall of her chest. Ellen Phillips. The name was Ellen Phillips. And it wasn't just anyone's name. It was hers.

But it wasn't hers.

She massaged her temples. This was so confusing. How could she be someone, but not be someone.

Run, a little voice in her head taunted. *Don't let him find you.*

Run where, and from who?

This was all wrong. Detective Petroski couldn't protect her. She didn't know how she knew. She just knew that she had to get away from him. She had to go somewhere where no one, not even the police, would think to look for her.

But where?

She had to do something soon. The longer she waited, the further they were from anything familiar. She wasn't sure where he was taking her, only that it was somewhere outside of Twin Oaks. They'd passed the city limit five minutes ago.

"I haven't eaten yet today," she told Petroski. "Do you mind if we stop?"

"Can't it wait?" He looked at his watch. "It's noon. Everything will be packed and we're kind of in a rush."

That's what she was betting on. "Low blood sugar," she said. "If I don't eat I get really sick and pass out. Didn't Detective Thompson tell you?"

He looked over to her, then back at his watch, and sighed heavily. "Fine, but let's make it quick."

He pulled into the first fast-food place that came along, cursing when he saw that the line for the drive-thru stretched all the way out to the street.

"Why don't we just go in and order the food?" she offered. "I have to use the ladies' room, anyway."

"Yeah, okay." The lot was nearly full so he swung into a handicapped spot next to the door.

As they stepped inside, the aroma of grease and old coffee turned her stomach. No way she would be able to force down food right now. The idea of eating anything tossed her already unsettled stomach.

All the lines inside were four and five people long, and Petroski swore. "This is gonna take an hour."

"I'll use the bathroom while you wait," she told him, inching away.

He grabbed her by the arm. "Hold on. I don't know if that's such a great idea."

"Come on," she said. "What could happen to me in a crowded restaurant? Besides, I really have to go."

She did a knee cross to drive the point home.

Finally, he relented. "Come right back. Hey, what do you want me to order for you?"

"Anything is fine," she called over her shoulder. She wouldn't be eating it anyway.

She rounded the corner and headed for the bathroom, but stopped just outside the door. She stood there, out of his line of sight, waiting for several minutes before rushing back. He'd moved up two people in line.

"I've got a problem," she told him. At his quizzical look, she added quietly, "A *feminine* problem."

He looked perplexed for a second, then recognition dawned. "Oh, right. So can't you take care of it?"

"The machine in the rest room is empty. I have stuff in my bag, but it's locked in the car."

The person in front of them was giving their order and Petroski looked anxiously to the counter. "Can't you wait? I'm gonna lose my spot in line."

She shifted from foot to foot. "I'm not sure how long the TP is going to hold, if you know what I mean."

He looked thoroughly grossed out, just as she had hoped he would. He pulled his keys out and handed them to her. "Here, go get what you need. Just be careful, okay? Come right back."

She snatched the keys from his hand, forcing herself to sound perky. "It'll just take me a second!"

Yeah, she thought as she headed out the door, a second to grab her stuff and go.

Mitch sat at his desk, nursing a Coke and fighting a killer headache. He'd been trying to convince himself all morning that Jane would be fine, and that he'd done the right thing—the responsible thing—by passing her case over to someone else.

But if he was so sure of himself, why did he feel so damned guilty?

"Detective!"

Mitch looked up to see Officer Greene walking toward him, file in hand.

"We got a hit on a missing-person report. It's Jane."

Mitch's heart jumped up into his throat. "Let me see it."

Greene handed him the file. "The report was filed in Lincoln Heights. A co-worker reported her missing when she didn't show up. She said they do 'sensitive' work and she was concerned when her friend didn't get in touch with her."

There was a copy of the report, and a computer print-out of a driver's license. Jane's driver's license. With Jane's picture.

Not Jane. Ellen Phillips.

"The mystery is solved."

"Not exactly," Greene said. "When I got her name I did some digging. Look at the next page."

He quickly scanned the next page. Aw, hell. He was afraid of something like this. "What kind of work did you say they do?"

"The desk over in Lincoln said the woman wouldn't go into detail. But she said she was pretty sure this friend of hers was in trouble. Said it wasn't like her not to check in."

No doubt it was something illegal. He'd bet his badge on it.

Damn. This was not a good sign.

His phone rang and he snatched it up from the cradle answering gruffly, "What."

He listened for several minutes to Petroski shout and curse on the other end, barely comprehending what he was hearing. Oddly enough, his first reaction was to laugh, then when he thought about it for a minute, he just wanted to wring Jane's—make that Ellen's or whoever the hell she was—neck. He'd been right, she was up to something, but he'd never expected this. Not even from her.

"I'll take care of it," he told Petroski before he slammed down the phone. What little harness he had left on his anger was swiftly slipping away.

He stuffed the paper back into the file and grabbed his cuffs from the top drawer of his desk. "I have to go."

"Trouble, Detective?"

"You could say that. I have to go and arrest our friend Ellen."

"Arrest her? What for?"

"She just stole a police car."

Chapter 14

Mitch pulled up in front of his mother's house, not at all surprised to see Detective Petroski's car parked in the driveway. Up until that very moment, he wasn't sure he really believed it. But he knew that if he would find Jane anywhere, it would be here. She didn't know anyone else.

What the hell had she been thinking?

He came to a screeching halt, tore the keys from the ignition and vaulted out of the car, stomping his way to the front door. He tried the handle but it was locked, so he used his key. The door unlocked with no problem, but when he tried to open it, it wouldn't budge. He pounded with a balled fist. "Lisa, open up!"

He got no answer, so he stalked around the house to try the back door. Through the sheer curtains in the window of the door, he could see a chair hooked under the knob.

He shook his head. This was friggin' unbelievable. They'd barricaded themselves into the house. Did they really think that would keep him out?

He slammed his fist into the door. "Damn it, Lisa, open this door, or I swear to God I'll shoot it down!"

"Go away," a muffled voice called. "We don't need you to protect her anymore. She's staying with us now."

"I'm not here to protect her. I'm here to arrest her." He didn't get a response. "Open the damned door. Don't make me call for backup."

Lisa's face appeared in the window over the kitchen sink. "She didn't steal that car. She was only borrowing it. He gave her the keys."

"You know as well as I do that he didn't give her the keys so she could drive off with his vehicle."

"In that case, she's going to plead insanity. It was a side effect of the head injury. She didn't know what she was doing."

He glared up at her, shading his eyes from the sun with the file. "You see this? This is a file on a certain Jane Doe. Also known as *Ellen Phillips*."

There was a pause then, "So."

"Why don't you sound surprised?"

He heard muffled voices, then, "You promise to be nice to her?"

"Nice?"

"You have to promise not to yell at her or make her feel bad. You've done enough already, don't you think?"

"Meaning what?"

Lisa glared down at him. "Meaning, maybe you should have kept your gun in the holster where it belonged."

Son of a—

If Lisa knew, that meant his mother probably knew, too. Great.

"I promise I'll be nice," he said through gritted teeth. After he'd arrested Jane—Ellen—*whoever*—he was arresting his sister for obstruction and harboring a fugitive. And for pissing him off.

He saw Lisa's shadow through the curtain, heard the doorknob rattle as she pulled the chair away. He twisted the knob and shoved the door open. "Jane," he shouted. "Where are you?"

Lisa stood next to the door, arms folded over her chest. "That won't work. You have to be nice to her or she won't come out."

"Ellen Phillips," he called.

She appeared in the hallway, his mother close behind her. "You know my name."

"Apparently you do, too."

She nodded. "It all started coming back a little while ago. It's still kind of jumbled in my head, but for the most part, I remember everything."

"That's good," Mitch said, tossing the file on the kitchen table. "Because I want you to tell me who the hell you *really* are."

"I guess I owe you an explanation," Ellen said. And she didn't have a clue where to begin. There was so much to say. While she drove to Mitch's mom's, memories had begun to flood through her mind. Including a lot of things she'd have been better off forgetting forever. It's no wonder she couldn't remember who she was, what with two people in there throwing clues at her.

Everything was still a little jumbled up there and she was having some trouble keeping her two lives separate in her mind.

"Go ahead." Mitch settled into one of the kitchen chairs. "I'm all ears. And if I like what I hear, I may not arrest you."

"I only borrowed that car."

"I'm not talking about the car. I'm talking about fraud. About the identity you stole, because I have to tell ya, *Ellen*, you look pretty good for someone who died of leukemia twenty years ago."

She bit her lip, cringing at his sharp tone, but he had every right to be angry. Just as he deserved her anger in return. "Don't get all self-righteous on me, Detective. At least I didn't knowingly lie to you. And I can explain everything."

The cop facade didn't waver an inch. "Somehow I knew you were going to say that."

"But first I need to use the phone. I've been trying to call someone and haven't been able to get ahold of her. It's imperative I talk to her."

"Absolutely not."

Mitch's mother placed a protective hand on her shoulder. "Mitch, where are your manners. Of course she can use the phone."

"Mother, I don't think—"

Every bit of patience drained from her voice. "She's been missing for three days and there are people out there who are worried about her. Let her make the damned call."

He sank back into the chair and mumbled, "Fine. You have five minutes."

Lisa handed her the phone and Ellen dialed the number of the shelter again. Please be there, she prayed. There was no way he could have found Anna, too.

When Ellen had gone to the police department to meet Detective Thompson, then followed him to the store, she'd had the feeling she was being followed. She'd told Anna, her assistant, as much when she'd called her from her car.

Her car. Where had her car gone? she wondered. And her cell phone. She had to get home, see what he'd done. He would have been looking for information, which meant her house would have been thoroughly tossed. It wouldn't be the first time, or the last.

"Hello," Anna answered, her voice guarded. Ellen went weak with relief. Anna had only been with them for a few months and was still nervous most of the time. Always edgy. Some women never got over the fear of being discovered.

"Anna, it's me."

"Oh, thank God. Oh, Ellen, I was so scared. I thought for sure something horrible happened to you. I know I shouldn't have called the police but I was so afraid."

So that's how Mitch knew her name. "It's okay, Anna, you did the right thing. But I need to know about the woman that called Friday. Did she come to the shelter? Is she okay?"

"When you disappeared she got scared. I haven't heard from her since Saturday night."

Ellen dropped her head in her hand, swore softly. There was no way they would find the woman now.

"I tried to get her to come in. I even called that Detective she told us about."

"You called the station?"

"No, she gave me his home number. But don't worry, I did like you showed me and blocked the call. But he didn't answer. I got his machine, and I was afraid to leave a message."

The blocked call they'd gotten Saturday night at Mitch's house. It had been Anna. If he had only answered the phone—

Across the room, Mitch cleared his throat loudly.

"Anna, I have to go. I just wanted to let you know that I'm okay. I'll call you later and fill you in on everything that happened."

They said goodbye and Ellen handed the phone back to Lisa.

Mitch stood and motioned to the door. "Let's go."

Lisa stepped in front of her. "No way. You promised not to arrest her."

"Promises don't mean much to him," Ellen said, her voice dripping with venom. Mitch looked appropriately wounded by her statement, but instead of satisfying some sense of vengeance, she felt rotten for hurting him.

"I'm not arresting her." He pushed Lisa aside and hooked a hand under Ellen's arm. "*Yet.* I'm going to take her outside where we can get a little privacy."

"It's okay, Lisa," Ellen assured her. "I have a lot to tell him."

Mitch turned to his sister. "Do me a favor and call the station, ask for Petroski and tell him I have his car."

"Is he mad?" Ellen asked and swore she could see the hint of a smile on Mitch's face.

"Yeah, he's mad. Probably humiliated more than anything."

Mitch led her outside, to the picnic table. The afternoon sun warmed her arms and shoulders, chasing away the chill that had gripped her since her memories returned and she realized the predicament she was in.

She sat on the bench and Mitch sat beside her, a few feet away.

"So tell me," he said. And just like that, he'd slipped into cop mode, his voice—his expression—completely devoid of emotion. "And I want the truth."

She clasped her hands, rubbing her palms together. "Ellen is obviously not my real name."

"No kidding."

She tried to ignore the sarcasm, but it still stung. "I stole her name when I went underground. My real name—" She paused. How long had it been since she'd spoken her own name? If she told Mitch—if she told anyone—it was possible her husband would find her. She wasn't sure if she was ready to take that chance. "I don't use my real name anymore."

"It would be in your best interest to tell me what your real name is."

"If I tell you, it could put my life in danger."

"The healed fractures? The scars?"

The words were nearly impossible to force out. "It was…my husband."

"You mean ex-husband?"

She shook her head.

"You're married," he said and cursed under his breath. "Christ, could this get any better."

"Only on paper. In my heart I ended our marriage the day I left."

"That doesn't make it any less legal." Anger leaked into his tone. "It doesn't change the fact that I've been messing around with someone's wife."

"You make it sound cheap. It wasn't like that and you know it. If I could have gotten a divorce I would have. He would have rather seen me dead. My only option was to escape, to start over."

"Tell me," he said. "What did he do to you? I need to hear it."

"He nearly destroyed me." Her voice wavered. The memory of the terror her husband had put her through was still hard to talk about, to think about. Even when her memory was gone, she'd felt him lurking somewhere in the farthest corner of her mind, taunting her. "He...he would beat me, and he would toy with me. He'd say things like, 'do you know how easy it would be to kill you. All I have to do is put a pillow over your face while you're sleeping,' or 'I could snap your neck like a twig, toss you down the stairs and no one would ever know.'"

"What about your family? Why didn't they help you?"

"He had everyone fooled. My parents adored him. After a particularly vicious beating—I think for something as trivial as leaving a microscopic wrinkle in one of his work shirts—I finally mustered the courage to tell them the truth. They accused me of being spoiled and ungrateful."

Mitch swore again.

"Their assumption wasn't completely without merit. The truth is, I was more than a little wild as a teenager. I had no direction. I didn't do well in school. I rebelled against everything and everyone that I could. My attitude got me fired from every job I ever worked."

Mitch shook his head and mumbled, "No wonder you and Lisa get along so well."

"My parents thought Mark was a godsend. They were thrilled when I got married. It seemed I had found some sort of purpose, something I was good at—becoming the perfect little housewife."

"All the broken bones... There must have been bruises. Didn't they notice?"

"He was careful to not hit me where my clothing wouldn't cover the evidence. The times things were broken, or I had a visible bruise, he'd write it off as me being a klutz. I tripped on the stairs, or slipped and hit my head while I was washing the kitchen floor. My parents were more than happy to play along if it meant keeping balance in their perfect world. My mom would laugh it off and say things like, 'Oh, she's always been accident prone.'"

"Were you?"

"Until I married him, I'd never broken a bone. I'd never even had stitches. Convincing herself that it was my fault, that I was the one with the problem, was her way of shutting out reality."

"But you left him. You got away."

Talking about it, remembering each horrible detail brought back every bit of pain, every ounce of resentment. But none of it came close to what she'd felt those last few days—the agony that had finally given her the strength to run away.

"I had to leave him," she said, feeling as hollow and cold inside as she had that day. "He stole my baby from me."

Mitch curled his hands into tight fists, wondering just how much worse this could get. If her husband beat the kid, too, if he'd taken the kid away from Jane—Ellen—Mitch would have to find the guy and do some serious damage. And he *would* find him. "You have a child?"

"Could have had. *Should* have had, but he took that from me, too." The pain in her eyes was as stark and fresh as if it had happened yesterday. "I was under the delusion that if I could be perfect, if I could wear the right clothes, keep the house clean enough, say all the right things, that someday he would be satisfied. I thought that day had come when I found out I was pregnant."

A soft breeze lifted the hair back from her face. She was so beautiful, yet filled with so much sadness. What should have been a happy memory only seemed to bring her sorrow. And he ached with her. He felt helpless to make it all better. There was no way to fix this.

And damn it, he wanted to fix it.

She took a deep breath and continued. "We'd been trying to get pregnant for almost two years with no luck. When that test came up positive, I was so excited. I was sure he would change. I mean, what kind of man would hit the mother of his child."

"He didn't change?" Mitch asked and she shook her head.

"Not only did he not change, the beatings became more severe. He would actually threaten to punch me in the stomach, then go on a rampage if I cried. He was really good at making me cry. Then I got sick. Really sick, and that wasn't allowed in our house. I've kept functioning through the worst cases of flu. I've cooked dinner and washed laundry with a temperature of one-hundred-and-four degrees. This was like nothing I'd ever had before. I remember hanging over the toilet vomiting until my whole body ached from dry heaves and fever. All the while he stood behind me, screaming at me to stop. Like I had some sort of control over what was happening to me. He threatened to kill my baby, to kill my parents. He went berserk. But I was so sick, I just wanted to die. I wanted it to finally be over with. I *wanted* him to kill me."

Mitch stared at his hands, taking it all in, slowly shaking his head. He couldn't let himself picture her that way. Not his Jane, she was too strong for that. She was too good a person, with too much spirit. She deserved to have everything her heart desired. She deserved to be happy. "But he didn't kill you."

"Almost. He kicked me hard in the stomach. The last thing I remember is an explosion of pain in my side, then everything went black."

"Your appendix," Mitch said. "The doctor said you had an appendectomy scar."

She nodded. "It burst. I woke up in the hospital the next day. They saved me, but I lost the baby."

"In your sleep, you said 'he took my baby.' That's what you meant." It explained the strange nightmares.

The bastard had taken her baby, and just like in her dream, no one had helped her. Someone should have seen it. Someone should have done something.

"Everything changed after that," she said. "I went numb inside. I finally realized that our marriage had never been about love. He thrived off control and manipulation. I would never be able to make him happy. He was his happiest, his most satisfied, when he was terrorizing me.

"Then I knew, it was kill or be killed. And since I could never kill another human being, even one as vile as him, I left. The night before I was supposed to be released from the hospital, I waited until he went home, packed the few things I had with me, walked away from the hospital, and never looked back. That was almost three years ago."

"And all this time he's never found you?"

"Twice he tracked me down. Both times I was lucky enough to get away. But I was running out of money, and places to hide. Then I learned about W.I.N.— Women In Need."

"I've heard of it. It's like an underground railroad for abused women."

"They got me my new identity, helped me relocate. I don't doubt for a second that they saved my life. Since then I've devoted myself to helping other women like me."

"That's what started this whole mess. You're hiding someone." The way someone had hidden her. He'd suspected—everything had pointed to that—but he hadn't wanted to believe it.

"The diapers, the baby food, they were for her kids."

"You know that what you're doing is illegal."

"What I do is necessary. These are women who have no other options."

Mitch glanced up at her. She looked weary and defeated, as if the weight of the world rested on her shoulders. "Where do *I* fit into all of this?"

"The woman that called the shelter where I work, she was hiding from her husband. She gave me your name, asked me to call you and set up a meeting."

"Is it someone I know?"

"She wouldn't tell us her name. She just said that she needed to see you, but she couldn't risk calling herself. She said she and her kids were in danger."

"What did she look like? How old were her kids?"

"I never actually saw her. We only talked on the phone long enough for her to give me your number."

"How many kids does she have?"

Ellen shrugged. "She wouldn't tell me. She only said that she would need diapers and baby food. Maybe we can figure out who it is. Is there anyone you know with kids? Someone that you would suspect of abuse. She had your home number, Mitch. That blocked call we got the other night was my assistant trying to get ahold of you. It would have to be someone you're friends with, right?"

Mitch scrubbed a hand across his jaw. "I know lots of people with kids. Darren has kids, Greene has a couple of kids. But would I suspect them of abusing their wives? Hell, no. Darren is like a brother to me. I would know if he was beating his wife. And Greene, well, he's a great guy. A good cop." But how well did Mitch really know him? Sometimes he was almost *too* nice.

"It'd be real easy to find out. Just call their houses and see if their wives are home."

"I can call the station and get Greene's number." He pulled out his cell phone, dialed the station, and within a few minutes was dialing Greene's home number. His wife answered. Mitch feigned an excuse for calling, then hung up. "It's definitely not her. She sounded fine, if not a little overwrought. I could hear a baby screaming in the background."

"What about Darren's wife."

"Diane? She's out of town."

Ellen sat straighter, eyes widening.

"It's not what you think. Her mother had a heart attack. Diane went to Washington to help her out until she gets back on her feet. She's had heart problems for years."

"How can you be sure?"

"I'm telling you, I know these people like family. I've never seen so much as a scratch on Diane. As far as I know she's never had a broken bone."

"Does she ever dress out of season? You know, long-sleeve shirts or turtlenecks on a hot summer day?"

"Never."

"She never seems afraid of him?"

Mitch laughed. "Are you kidding? I've seen her really lay into him. If anything, I'd say he's more afraid of her than she's ever been of him. Though he likes to pretend otherwise, she wears the pants in that family."

Jane—*Ellen*, would he never get used to that?—chewed on her thumbnail. "Then you're right, it's probably not her."

"What I really want to know is why you were following me that night."

"I called the station a couple of times that day but they kept telling me you were unavailable."

"I was interrogating Robbie. It went on most of the day and part of the night before."

"The officer at the desk said you'd just left, so I wrote down my number, said it was urgent that you get in touch with me. But when I went outside, I saw you walking to your car."

"How did you know it was me?"

"Someone yelled, 'Nice arrest, Thompson.' You turned and waved. I put two and two together."

"Why didn't you approach me right there?"

"Honestly, I didn't know if I could trust you. What I do isn't legal. Since I knew what you looked like, I could watch you from a distance. I wanted to follow you for a little while. Maybe strike up a casual conversation, get to know you first."

"So you followed me to the store."

"And someone was following me."

He heard a waver in her voice. She was scared, and trying like hell not to let it show. "We'll get him."

"We. There's a term you use rather loosely." She stared at the ground. "You promised me we would solve my case together. You said I wasn't alone."

"I also promised to keep you safe. I couldn't do that anymore."

"You mean you didn't want to."

"I was too close. If I had to do it all over again, I would do the same thing. I would rather have you alive and hat-

ing my guts than even think about someone hurting you."
Mitch reached over and slipped his hand over hers.

She looked down at their hands twined together,
filled with an emptiness so deep, so encompassing, she
ached clear through to her bones. For the first time in
three years she'd let someone close. She'd let him in,
only to have him push her away. "I really thought we
had a chance."

"Now you don't?"

"We stand on opposite sides of the law."

"If you wanted to, you could change that. You could
start by telling me your name." When she didn't answer,
Mitch dropped her hand. "But, I guess that's not a sacrifice you're willing to make."

Anger burned in her cheeks. "Don't talk to me about
sacrifices, Mitch. You have no idea what I've given up.
For more than three years I wasn't allowed to think for
myself, I couldn't say what I was feeling. That ended
the night I walked out of that hospital. I swore I would
never let anyone control me again. If I feel something,
damn it, I'm going to express it. If I want to do something, I do it."

"So what? I should give up being a cop for you. I
should hand over my badge and throw all my principles
out the window—"

"No. I would never ask you to do that. You already
rank a close second to me in the sacrifices department."

Now he sounded angry. "You have some sort of problem with my family?"

"No, I think your family is great. I think *you're* the
one with the problem."

"Loving my family, wanting to take care of them— you think that's a problem? That's pretty good coming from someone who's spent the last three years running away from hers."

"I don't have a choice—"

"*Everyone* has a choice." He stood, towering over her—an intimidating gesture, yet she knew deep down he would never hurt her. Not physically. He could break her heart though, but only if she let him.

"You can't run forever, Ellen. Some day, you're going to have to face your husband. No matter how far and how fast you go, eventually your past will catch up with you."

"Now you're talking like a cop."

Every bit of emotion disappeared from his voice. "I am a cop."

Ellen rose to her feet, meeting his challenging glare. "Then why don't we get this over with, Detective. Do what you came here to do."

Mitch reached behind him, grabbing his cuffs from the back of his belt. "Ellen Phillips, you're under arrest."

Chapter 15

Mitch sat at his desk, staring at the computer screen, seeing nothing. He had reports to type, work to do, and he couldn't concentrate on a damned thing.

"Uncle Mitch!"

He swiveled toward the voice to see a streak of blond headed his way. Jessica, Darren's daughter, vaulted into his arms. Talk about a mood lifter. "Hey kiddo, what are you doin' here. You looking for a job?"

Jessica giggled and wrapped two skinny arms around his neck, planting a big, sloppy kiss on his cheek. "I'm too little to work, silly."

"Don't you have a birthday coming up?"

She gave him an exasperated look. "I'm only gonna be *five*."

He feigned a serious look. "You look more like eight or nine to me."

"And she acts twenty-five." Darren walked in, his youngest, Lauren, balanced on his hip. She had the same wispy blond hair as her sister, and enormous blue eyes. Both girls were the spitting image of Darren.

Jessica bounded off Mitch's lap, hopping excitedly at her father's feet. A little blond ball of energy. "Daddy, can I play the game on your computer? Pleeeze. Pretty pleeeze."

"For a few minutes. Take your sister with you. I need to talk to Uncle Mitch for a minute." He handed the baby over and like an expert, Jessica propped her on her hip and bounded off for her father's desk.

"How's it goin'?" Darren swung into the chair next to Mitch's desk, straddling the back. "From the looks of it when you brought Ellen in today, maybe things didn't go so well?"

And now Darren had come to say I-told-you-so. As if Mitch didn't feel rotten enough already. "She didn't resist arrest, if that's what you mean."

"I heard she wouldn't give you her real name."

"Nope." All that talk about trusting him had been exactly that. Talk. When it came right down to it, she didn't trust him at all. And could he blame her?

"I heard that place she works for hired some bigwig lawyer from Detroit to represent her. He's posting bail as we speak. He argued that giving her real name would put her in mortal danger. She'll probably walk on all charges."

"What about police protection?"

"She doesn't want it," Darren said. "She thinks the guy after her has probably given up by now since his wife is long gone."

"What do you think?"

"I think she's probably right. But I'm going to take her home, check her place out first, make sure no one is waiting for her."

"*You're* going to take her home?"

"Look, I feel guilty for the way I handled things." He scrubbed a hand across his cheek. Mitch realized suddenly that Darren hadn't shaved. In fact, his best friend looked like hell.

"What's going on, Darren?"

"The truth? I was jealous. I was jealous that you were happy when my life is falling apart. The fact is, Diane is leaving me."

"Leaving you? Darren, what are you talking about? You guys have a great marriage."

"I thought so, too, but she lied to me about her mother. She didn't go to Washington."

Mitch was stunned to see a deep blush burn a path up Darren's throat and into his cheeks. Darren who was always in control, always cool. "Then, where is she?"

"She left me for another man. She dropped the kids back home yesterday and took off. I have no idea how I'm going to explain it to them."

Mitch sat back, stunned. "That's, wow…I never would have expected this."

"Neither did I. At first she gave me some crap about needing to find herself, but when I pushed her a little, she admitted there was someone else. I came by yesterday to talk to you about it, but when I saw you and Jane together, looking so happy, I couldn't do it."

Looking happy?

And he had been, he realized. Being with her the past couple of days made him feel alive again.

"I slept with her." The words fell out of his mouth unexpectedly, but Darren didn't look surprised. "I swore I wouldn't, but I just couldn't stop myself."

"Are you in love with her?"

"I don't know. Maybe I am."

"Did you tell her?"

"There's no point. I'm a cop and what she does for a living is illegal. Being with me would mean having to give that up. She won't make that sort of sacrifice for anyone." Damn, he sounded like a lovesick kid. Three days he'd known her. Three short days, yet it felt like a lifetime.

"Detective Waite, are you ready to take me home?"

Mitch's head snapped up while his heart simultaneously sank straight down to his toes. Jane—Ellen— was standing behind him. And she'd probably just heard every word he'd said. Christ, could he make himself look a little more pathetic? But instead of feeling humiliation, anger coursed through him.

Jane was right. He spent too damned much time and energy taking care of other people, sacrificing himself at his own expense. Now, when he finally wanted something for himself, he was denied that, too.

Apparently Darren hadn't noticed Jane either because he looked just as startled by her presence. He pushed himself up from the chair, clearing his throat.

"Uh, yeah, sure. I just have to drop the girls at my mother's house. You're sure this is what you want to do."

"I'm sure." Her chin lifted a defiant notch. "I can take care of myself."

Darren backed away. "I'm just going to grab the girls and wait outside while you two tie things up."

"There's nothing to tie up." Mitch turned away from Jane, away from everything that was good in his miserable life. "We've said everything there is to say."

His cell phone rang and he used it as an excuse to dismiss them both, to not turn around and watch her walk out of his life. And when he finally did turn to look, they were gone.

"Brother dear," Lisa said sweetly, when he answered. "I need you to run to the store for me."

Great, just what he needed. As if his day wasn't bad enough, he'd have to spend his afternoon running errands for his sister. He grabbed a pen and a pad of paper. "What do you need?"

"Mom's running low on painkillers. I called the pharmacy for a refill."

"Lisa, the pharmacy is three blocks away. Can't you *walk* there and pick them up?"

"And leave Mom? I disappear for two minutes and she's up moving around. Suppose she falls."

"Fine," he grumbled. "I'll get the pills."

"Oh, and I need a few things from the grocery store."

She rattled off a list, but somewhere between the peanut butter and the toilet paper, Mitch's mind began to wander. He started to think about the long recovery his mother had ahead of her, and all the trips to the store he would be making. And the weekly trips to her house to cut the grass. And Lisa—Christ, he was getting sick of worrying about when she was going to grow up and take charge of her own life.

Jane's voice echoed in his head. *Technically, the only thing stopping Lisa from the career of her choice is you.*

Maybe he was holding her back, but he was doing it because he loved her. If he gave her the money, he would constantly be worried about her choices. About seeing her fail. Because he knew she'd had so much bad luck in her life, one more failure might be the blow that finally did her in.

But honestly, by holding onto her money, by holding her back, was he worrying any less now? Was she any happier?

Then he thought about Jane's husband. What had she told Mitch? She wasn't allowed to think for herself, she couldn't say what she was feeling. Was what Mitch had done to Lisa any less reprehensible? Though he'd like to believe otherwise, he was controlling her, just as Jane's husband had controlled her.

"Mitch!" Lisa shouted in his ear and Mitch jumped in his seat. "Hello. Have you heard a single thing I've said?"

"Sorry, no. I wasn't listening."

"Are you going to the store for me or not?"

"Not."

There was a silence, then, "What do you mean, *not?* Need I remind you that you're the one that wanted this little arrangement in the first—"

"Lisa, shut up. Do me a favor and call the doctor's office. Ask them if they could recommend a good service to find Mom someone to come and sit with her a couple of days a week."

"Not that I don't think that's a great idea, but I'm not sure if her insurance will cover it. It could cost a fortune."

"Don't worry about that. We'll find a way to pay for it. If you can find someone to stay with her during the day Monday through Friday, I'll take a couple of nights a week and one full weekend day."

"But, what about work? You can't commit yourself to this then back out—"

"Don't worry. I'll schedule around it. Also, the kid that lives across the street, he's what, twelve or thirteen?"

"Something like that."

"Ask him if he'd be interested in making a little cash every week. We need someone to do the lawn."

There was another long silence then Lisa said, "Mitch, you're scaring me."

"And, Lisa, one more thing."

"Why stop at one, you're on a roll."

"That guy, the one who owns the resort, tell him you'll have the money for the dog-grooming deal by the end of the month." There was no response this time, just a barely audible squeak on the other end of the line. "You're welcome."

For the first time in his life, he'd stunned his sister into silence. Hot damn.

He hung up the phone, feeling weightless, as if a tremendous load had been lifted from his shoulders. Then the gravity of what he'd just done hit full force.

By doing this, he was assuring himself time to sit

back and dwell on how lonely and pathetic his life had become. Time to spend alone—without Jane.

Then he had a revelation, one that nearly knocked him back in his chair. Had he unconsciously kept himself in a state of chaos with work and family to fill some void in his life? Is that what Jane had been trying to make him see? Without smacking him upside the head and saying look, idiot. Look what you've done to yourself. Instead she'd dropped little hints, pushed him into figuring it out for himself.

And he had. Only he'd figured it out too late.

And damn it, he missed her already.

"Detective?"

Mitch looked up to see Greene standing across the desk, dressed in his street clothes.

"I just wanted to let you know, I checked out all the guys on the force who I know have kids. Nothing panned out."

"Well, it was a long shot. We may never figure out who did it." He sighed and leaned back in the chair, feeling a kind of tired that settled in deep. "You off duty?"

"Yeah." Greene tugged a set of keys from the pocket of his jeans. "Gotta get home and rescue my wife. Kids are driving her nuts. The baby has a pretty nasty case of colic and my oldest is hell on wheels into his terrible twos."

It sounded like total chaos, and it sounded completely wonderful. Going home to a house full of kids, and a wife like Jane.

No, not just someone *like* Jane. He wanted the genuine article. He wanted long nights of making love to her and waking with her still in his arms. He wanted her face to be the last thing he saw before he went to sleep at night and the first thing he saw every morning. He wanted it all—the mortgage, the minivan, the sleepless nights pacing the floor because the baby was teething.

He wanted to make up for all the misery she'd been through, to show her that she couldn't lose faith in people. That he was different.

He wanted to make her happy.

And he'd let it slip through his fingers, because like Jane had said, they stood on either side of the law. There was no gray area for him.

"I'll see you later, Detective." Greene started to leave, then turned back. "By the way, someone called my house this afternoon. Talked to my wife. You wouldn't know anything about that, would you?"

It was pretty clear to Mitch that Greene already knew he'd made the call. He probably had caller ID. Mitch hadn't even thought about blocking the number.

"It was me," he told him. "I called."

"Because I have kids."

"It was nothing personal—"

"You don't have to explain. I know you were just doing your job. If I were in your position, I would have done the same thing."

"Yeah, but I don't…" He was going to say "have a family," but the words caught in his throat.

"Why don't you go home, Detective? You're not doing anyone much good here."

Mitch managed a sheepish grin. "I look that bad, huh?"

"Go home, take a day to think about it. Things will be clearer tomorrow."

"You know, that's the best advice I've had all day."

He gave a halfhearted wave as Greene walked out, then grabbed his sport coat from the back of his chair and slung it over his shoulder. Maybe a little bit of time to himself would help him think things through—make some sense of this mess and figure out what he was going to do to fix it.

He started out the door and made it halfway to his car before a short, plump woman with a careworn face intercepted him. He knew that face. He'd seen her in the station the other night, protesting her son's innocence.

"Detective Thompson," she said. "I'm Lorraine Barrett, Robby's mother."

"I'm sorry for your loss, Mrs. Barrett, but I have nothing to say to you." Mitch lengthened his stride, and she huffed along to keep up with him.

"You arrested my son. You interrogated him. I just want to know if you truly believed him to be guilty. I need to hear it from you."

Mitch pulled out his keys and unlocked his car. "Your son was a known sex offender."

Mrs. Barrett slapped a hand against his door, holding it shut. The desperation in her eyes, the pain, left Mitch feeling like a heartless bastard.

"I know my son was no angel, Detective. He had problems, but he was seeing a counselor. He was taking drugs to help control his urges. He wasn't violent. He wasn't capable of hurting those women."

As long as he didn't look at her, Mitch could walk away from this without saying or doing something monumentally stupid and irresponsible.

She seemed to sense that, because she got right in his face. "I believe you're an honest man, Detective. You wouldn't tell a grieving mother that her son was a monster unless you really believed it. So look me in the eye. Look me in the eye and tell me you think my son was guilty and I'll accept it. And I'll never bother you again."

Then Mitch did the stupidest thing he could have. He looked her in the eyes. They were the same dull brown as her son's, and filled with as much fear and pain. And all he could think about was the way Robby had sworn he was innocent, how he'd bawled like a baby and begged for his mother. He hadn't even had the sense, the intellectual capacity, to ask for a lawyer. And they'd taken advantage of that. They'd grilled him for hours.

Could Mitch stand there, look this woman in the eyes and lie to her?

"No," he said, finally. "I don't think Robby was guilty."

Her eyes filled with grateful tears, and for the first time that day Mitch felt as if he'd done the right thing.

"I think he was framed, Mrs. Barrett. Now I have to figure out a way to prove it."

Chapter 16

The best advice he'd had all day turned into Mitch's worst nightmare. At home, he had nothing to do but think. Think about how he'd driven an innocent man to suicide while the real suspect still walked around a free man. How trying to prove it would be next to impossible, and probably enough to end his career. And when he wasn't thinking about that, he was thinking of Jane. There wasn't a place in his house that didn't remind him of her. She'd only been there two days but her aura hung like a ghost, haunting him.

Her scent clung to the sheets of his bed along with the faint impression of her body where she'd slept. Strands of her hair tangled in his hairbrush and the robe lay on the floor next to the couch, discarded there the first time they'd made love.

Even after Kim, he hadn't felt anything close to this. This relentless, gnawing ache.

He grabbed his beer off the table and took a swig, realizing an instant before the warm brew hit his palate that he had accidentally grabbed the bottle from the day before. He nearly gagged at the bitter sting. He jumped up from the couch and dashed to the kitchen, spitting the foul fluid into the sink.

That was one really bad beer. It had tasted a little skunky yesterday, but if it hadn't spilled, he probably would have finished it. Now he was glad he hadn't.

He dumped out what was left of the bottle and was just about to turn the tap on to wash it down when he noticed something odd. He leaned over to get a closer look and saw white specks against the stainless steel, so tiny he could have easily overlooked it.

Somewhere in the back of his brain, a warning bell sounded. He pressed his fingers to a few of the specks and rubbed them together. They smeared like paste, and the bell in his brain began to scream.

"No way. Not in a million years." He lifted his fingers to his mouth, touching them lightly to his tongue. Bitter. Bitter like someone had ground something up and slipped it into his drink.

He leaned over the tap, filling his mouth with water, then spitting it out, repeating the process until the taste was gone. He probably hadn't ingested enough to do any damage, but until he found out exactly what he was dealing with, he wasn't taking any chances. What he really didn't understand was how it got there in the first place. Besides himself and Jane, the only other person who'd been over—

Reality socked him square in the chest.

Darren had been there. Darren had given him the beer, cleaned up the mess when it spilled. Darren's wife and kids were out of town....

No, it couldn't be him. Mitch would have known. Darren was his best friend. A brother.

But he couldn't deny the facts, either. Darren did have a similar physical build as the suspect. They were roughly the same height. And what had the victim of the second beating said? The guy smelled expensive. Darren always wore cologne.

And most importantly, he'd had easy access to the case file.

Mitch still didn't want to believe it. He clung to the slim chance that it was all just some weird coincidence. But he had to get ahold of Jane. He had to warn her. According to the file, she lived about thirty minutes away, which meant they were probably almost there by now. But the file hadn't had a phone number—he'd checked.

Mitch grabbed the cordless off the counter and dialed Darren's cell number. It rang several times, then he was switched to voice mail. Damn!

He dialed the precinct instead. When the desk sergeant answered, Mitch asked him who had been on desk Friday night.

"I was on until midnight."

"Someone came in to see me that night. A woman."

"The amnesia lady, yeah. She was in here. She came in a couple minutes after you left."

"This is extremely important. She said she left me a message. I *need* the phone number off that message."

"I don't have it anymore. I gave it to Detective Waite."

Mitch's heart froze in his chest. "Detective Waite? Why would you give it to him?"

"He stopped by the desk right after her and asked what she wanted. When I told him, he said he'd give you the message himself. I asked him about it the next day and he told me it was a fake name and number."

Darren had never delivered any message. In the squad room the following morning, he'd acted as if he'd never seen Jane before, yet he knew her name, her phone number. He'd known her identity the whole time.

The pieces of the puzzle began to fall into place and panic crept up, seizing his breath. Jane was with Darren now, and it might already be too late.

Ellen sat in the front seat of Darren's car, looking out the window at the landscape bordering I-75 North. A landscape so wonderfully familiar, it should have filled her with contentment. She was going home, back to her life, to her work. She should have been ecstatic, but all she felt was tired. Tired of hiding, tired of running, tired of pretending she was living her life when really she'd only been in limbo. But most of all, she was tired of being lonely. For the first time in three years she was thinking that maybe she'd found a man she could trust. A man she could let herself love. A man worth the risk.

"He'll get over it," Darren said.

She turned to him. He'd been quiet for most of the trip, which had suited her just fine. "Who will get over what?"

"Mitch. He seems like he's really hurting, but he'll get over it. He always bounces back."

"Always? Are you implying that he goes through this sort of thing often?"

"You look pretty broken up. I just want you to know that he'll be okay when you're gone."

"Well, thanks. That makes me feel so much better." She breathed a silent sigh of relief as the sign for her exit appeared on the right. Maybe Darren was honestly trying to make her feel better. Maybe he didn't realize how tactless and insensitive he sounded. Or maybe he was deliberately trying to make her feel awful.

That being the case, it had worked.

Either way, she was glad their time together was about to end. "This is my exit," she said.

When he didn't switch lanes or even put on his turn signal, she thought maybe he hadn't heard her and said it louder. "You want to get off here. This is my exit."

He stared ahead, like she hadn't even spoken, and the exit whooshed past.

"Is there a problem?" she asked, hoping he couldn't hear the apprehension in her voice.

"No problem. We have time to kill."

A chill, like icy fingers, crawled up her spine. "Time for what?"

"You know, if you had just let Petroski take you to that motel, it would have been so much easier. Now I've had to change all my plans."

Plans? What was he talking about?

Something was very wrong with this picture. "I'd like to go home now."

"I hope you appreciate all of the trouble I've gone through for you." He glanced over, regarding her like she was a naughty child. "You haven't made this easy for me."

This time when she spoke, there was no doubt her voice was shaking. "And what trouble was that?"

"Planning your family reunion…Jill."

Jill? She swallowed back the panic clawing its way up her throat and forced herself to speak. "You know my real name."

"I know everything about you. You're Jillian Stone. Born and raised in northern California. Reported missing three years ago by your husband, David Stone." He looked over at her and grinned. Her blood ran cold. Pure evil lurked behind his smile. An evil she was all too familiar with.

"How?" she asked, her voice barely audible.

"How did I figure it out? I found your secret hiding place, in the wall, behind the dryer. Took me half a day of searching. I give you points for creativity."

Oh, God.

It had been Darren all along. He'd followed her into the store and attacked her. He'd stolen her purse and searched her house.

"Once I knew where you were from, it wasn't hard to find your family."

She tried to swallow, but her throat closed tight. "My husband, you didn't—"

"Call him? As a matter of fact, I did. He was so relieved to hear that you're okay. Ironically, all this time, he's been under suspicion for your disappearance. He hopped right on a plane to come get you so he can clear his name."

He would be beyond furious. And it would have been festering for three long years. There was no telling what he might do to her. Fear threatened to swallow her up. "Why? Why would you do that?"

"He's part of the plan. The game is almost over."

Her first instinct was to run, but she was trapped. She glanced at the door. They were going way too fast. She would never survive the jump, but if she could get him to slow down, maybe she could get away. She could flag down a passing car—

"I wouldn't try it," he said, and she glanced over at him, saw the glint of metal he held in his lap. He had a gun. And from the looks of it, not just any gun.

"I found this in your house, too." He shot her a disapproving look. "Shame on you, keeping an unregistered, loaded firearm in your house. You can get in trouble for that."

"You're absolutely right," she agreed. "Take me to the nearest police station and I'll turn myself in."

Darren laughed. It was a vile sound that vibrated through her like a cold chill. "You're tough. I like that about you. The tough ones are always the most fun to break."

"Mitch told me your wife is tough. Did you break her, too?"

He pointed the gun at her, digging the barrel into her cheek. She went stock-still.

"There will be no more disparaging comments about my wife." The metal sank deeper into her skin, to the point of pain. "I love her. She just needed to learn her place."

She nodded and he lowered the gun to his lap. She let out the breath she'd been holding and said a silent prayer of thanks.

She chose her next words carefully. "Why did she come to me for help?"

"I can't have her telling everyone what happened. I tried to explain, but she didn't understand."

He spoke of her in the present tense, which could mean that his wife was still alive. Or it could mean that he was completely nuts. He wasn't making a whole lot of sense.

Maybe that was the key to this. Running wasn't an option and overpowering him would probably get them both killed. Maybe she could try to reason with him.

"You're a cop," she said, hoping to appeal to his sense of duty. If crazy people could have a sense of duty. "Think of your career. Your little girls. You could get help. Counseling—"

"Blah, blah, blah." He rolled his eyes. "You act like this is my fault. You did this to yourself. If by some chance they find my wife's body, you'll recognize her. You'll put two and two together and where would I be then? No one can know."

His wife's body? He thought…? "But, I've only talked to your wife on the phone. I've never met her. I have no idea what she looks like. I didn't even know her name."

Darren looked over at her, let out a cackle of a laugh. "You're serious. You really didn't see her. Well, I guess this is your unlucky day. Killing you will just be a bonus."

"Mitch will figure it out. When I turn up dead—"

"My plan is foolproof. No one will ever figure it out."

His arrogance ignited a spark of anger and she embraced it. Anything to drown out the helplessness, the panic threatening to paralyze her. There had to be a way to outsmart him. And if that didn't work she would fight for her life. She would beat him, or she would die trying.

"You're awfully sure of yourself, aren't you?" she shot back. Her confidence, her anger, seemed to surprise him. "But no plan is foolproof. You'll be caught. It may take a year. Even two. But they'll catch you."

He looked over at her, studied her for so long she was sure he'd run them off the road. "I can see why Mitch fell in love with you. And you would have been good for each other. You would have been happy."

She knew he was only saying that to taunt her, but she knew without a doubt the words were true. She loved Mitch. If a person had a soul mate, an individual they were destined to be with above all others, Mitch was hers. And now she would probably never get the opportunity to tell him.

If she could somehow get a second chance, another shot, she would do anything to make it work. Even if that meant giving up her job, facing her past. He was worth the sacrifice.

"I think that's the first logical thing you've said today," she told Darren.

"Yeah. Too bad it will never happen."

It will if I can help it, she thought, a sudden rush of adrenaline coursing through her blood. She'd had enough. Enough of the hiding, the fear. It was time she took control of her life. *Real* control, and not the false sense of security she'd been hiding behind. Damn it, she wanted her life back.

There had to be a way out of this. She had to keep him talking, keep him distracted. "So tell me about this plan of yours. I mean, if I'm going to die I'd like to know how."

"If you're thinking you're going to get away and tell the police, think again."

She shrugged and looked out the window. "Fine, don't tell me. I'm probably better off not knowing anyway."

She never thought he'd fall for something so obvious as reverse psychology, but he took the bait.

"I was thinking a gunshot wound to the head. Fast and painless."

She suppressed a shudder. "How thoughtful of you."

"But not until your husband is through with you."

"You'll give my husband a crack at me, shoot me in the head, then what, you'll shake hands and go your separate ways? I thought he wanted to clear his name."

"You see, that's the beauty of it. He'll be dead, too. Your classic murder-suicide. The estranged husband finds his wife, shoots her, then shoots himself."

Terror threatened to overwhelm her. She had to stay focused. She had to work her way out of this.

"If Mitch loves me, and you're such a good friend, how can you justify killing me?"

"It's for his own good. He doesn't realize it now, but you're just like Kim. She used him. She almost ended his career. She's better off dead."

"You killed her, too?"

"I wish I had. She wanted to take Mitch down with

her. She was going to implicate him in her drug deals. She deserved what she got."

If he thought Kim deserved to die, that meant Jill didn't stand a chance.

Keep him talking. Keep him distracted.

"There's one thing I don't understand," she said. "How did you manage to abuse your wife with no one ever seeing a sign of it? There're always signs."

"I already told you, I love my wife. I never laid a finger on her. But she was nosy. She found my trophies, then she figured out what I'd done. She was going to tell the police if I didn't stop her."

"Trophies? What, like golf trophies?"

He turned to her, flashed that blood-chilling, evil smile. "From the girls. I always took two. One for myself and one to frame Robby Barrett."

Chapter 17

As Mitch sailed down I-75 to Jane's house, sirens wailing, his cell phone rang. And as it had every time since he'd alerted his sergeant and the state police, his heart lodged in his throat.

This time it was Greene. "I just talked to the Lincoln police. Her real name is Jill Stone."

Mitch's heart stalled in his chest. "They found her?"

"No, but we apprehended a David Stone. He claims to be her husband."

"Her husband? What the hell is he doing there?"

"Mr. Stone said a man called saying he'd found his missing wife and they made plans to meet at her house—Jane's house—but they haven't shown up yet. We cleared out and the local police have unmarked cars all over the place. If they show up, we'll spot them."

"Make sure they keep this Stone person in custody."

"It's been taken care of."

"They're maintaining radio silence? If Darren hears a call go out—"

"Don't worry, Detective, these guys know what they're doing. They'll find her. I—hang on a sec."

Mitch waited, hearing muffled voices in the background, like Greene had put his hand over the mouthpiece. "Come on, damn it," he mumbled, veering to avoid colliding with a semi. A few more miles and he'd be at the exit. He couldn't stop beating himself up over the fact that he hadn't figured it out sooner. If he'd only shelved his pride and driven her home himself…

Finally Green came back on the line. "They just searched Darren's house. They found Diane."

"Tell me she's alive."

There was a pause, then, "I'm sorry, sir."

Ah, Christ. How could Darren kill his own wife. The mother of his children. And he'd sat there, not an hour ago, straight-faced, and lied to Mitch. Said she'd run off with another man. What else had he lied about over the years?

And those poor little girls. What would happen to them? Jessica and Lauren would go through losing their mother, then their father.

All this time Darren had been abusing his wife and Mitch never suspected a thing. A week ago, he never would have believed it. Now, anything seemed possible.

"Detective, are you still there?"

"We have to contact Diane's mother," Mitch said, his voice faltering. He couldn't lose it. Not now. "We have to find out where Darren's kids are."

"It's being taken care of. We…hang on a sec."

While Mitch waited he thought about Kim, about walking into his apartment and finding her dead. At the time he'd felt oddly detached. Of course, he'd been sorry to see her life end, but he hadn't been heartbroken. Later, when it'd had time to sink in, he'd felt a deep sense of pity, mostly for her family. And a healthy dose of anger toward her for messing up his life.

This was different. If he didn't get to Jane in time and something happened to her, he knew without a doubt it would destroy him.

Greene was back on the line. "What's your present location, Detective?"

"I'm about a half-mile south of the Lincoln exit."

"We just got a call in from the state police. They got a hit on Darren's plate."

Mitch held his breath. Please, God, let it not be too late. "Where are they?"

"About ten miles north of you."

"North?"

"Her husband said he's supposed to meet them at seven. From what I can figure, Darren is stalling, so he'll get there right at seven o'clock."

Mitch slammed his foot down on the accelerator. "Which means I still have time to make it there before them."

"Is she dead?" Jill asked.

Darren almost looked remorseful. "I didn't want to kill her. I love her, but she was going to tell."

Jill swallowed a sob. She'd failed Darren's wife. She

hadn't been able to keep her safe. If only she'd been more careful. If she had just approached Mitch at the station. If she hadn't decided to follow him, none of this would have happened. Darren's wife would be alive and Darren would be in jail. "When they find her, they'll know it was you."

"They won't find her. I'm going to take her someplace no one will look." He shook his head. "This is her own fault. Always thinking she was so smart, so much better than me. And it was so easy to fool her."

"How did you find her?"

"See, that's the best part. She found me. She called me, asked me to turn myself in. I cried, told her I loved her, that I wanted to get help, that I *needed* her." He laughed. "She actually believed me. I told her I was going to turn myself in, but I couldn't do it without her. I needed her to take care of me. She fell right into my trap."

It seemed as though everyone had been underestimating Darren. He was a monster. And if she wasn't able to stop him, he would get away with it. Her death would be for nothing.

Darren looked at his watch and switched his turn signal on, veering toward the approaching exit. "It's almost time. He'll be waiting."

When they pulled into her driveway, it was empty. Maybe he hadn't come. Maybe David suspected something was up and decided not to show. Or maybe he called the police.

"Don't look so relieved," Darren said. "I told him not to park in the driveway. He's here."

A brief dash of hope was instantly smothered. There was no way out of this. She was going to die, and no one would ever know the truth.

Mitch would never how much she loved him.

"I'm going to get out and you're going to slide out after me. You're going to get out slowly and walk with me to the house. If you try anything, I'll shoot you in the stomach. You won't die right away, and you'll be in excruciating pain. Understand?"

She nodded.

He opened his door and climbed out, the gun tucked against his side and aimed at her. Trembling from the inside out, she slid across the seat. She was so weak with fear, she wasn't sure she would be able to make it to the front door. She wondered what he would do if she passed out.

Probably shoot her on principle.

As she stepped out of the car, she glanced quickly around to see if any of her neighbors were out. If she could somehow alert someone…but the neighborhood was eerily silent. The area was lower-middle class, and most people worked for a living. Not to mention that she didn't really know them. Part of being invisible was not making friends. No one would notice anything out of the ordinary, because no one knew what was ordinary for her.

"Let's go." He grabbed her forearm, digging his fingers into her skin. He led her to the front door, the gun jabbing her side. He was getting excited, like a little kid anticipating Christmas morning. He was looking forward to this.

Her stomach pitched and her knees felt wobbly. He

pushed open the front door and shoved her in, closing and locking it behind her.

The television was on, tuned in to some sports channel. The room was a wreck. He'd obviously done a thorough job of searching.

She heard a noise from the kitchen, her heart sinking low when she realized it was her husband in there. That any second he would walk out and three years' worth of hiding would be over. She would realize her greatest fear. In an odd way, it was almost a relief. The running would be over.

Her hands shook and her head felt dizzy. She swayed and Darren dug his fingers deeper into her arm.

"Oh, no you don't. You're going to be conscious for this. I can't wait to see the look on your face."

In the kitchen, she heard the sound of a drawer closing.

"Stone!" Darren called.

A figure appeared in the arch leading to the kitchen. She had to blink several times to be sure her eyes weren't deceiving her. It wasn't her husband standing there. It was Mitch.

"You can put away the weapon. I've already checked out the house. It's clear," he said. He didn't seem to notice Darren was pointing it at her.

"What are you doing here?" Darren asked.

"I told you I would let you know when we had more information. We learned Ellen's not the only name she stole. She's been a busy girl. She's wanted for fraud in three states. And kidnapping. I'm here to arrest her." He looked at Jill, his voice dripping with disdain. "I trusted you, and you lied about everything."

Jill was too stunned to speak. She had no idea what he was talking about. She'd never committed fraud or kidnapped anyone. Then she realized he was lying. He had somehow figured it out and he was there to save her. He was trying to get her away from Darren. She had to stay calm. She had to play along.

"Isn't that right, Jill?"

She let her mouth drop open and a small gasp escaped. He knew her name. That meant they'd probably apprehended her husband. But did he know about Robby? Did he know about Darren's wife?

Mitch took a step toward them. "The feds have been hot on your trail. Another day and they would have had you. But this is going to be my collar."

"Are you here alone?" Darren asked, the cool facade not slipping an inch.

"I didn't see much point calling for backup. Between the two of us I didn't figure there would be a problem arresting her."

The fingers on her arm tightened and Darren stiffened beside her. He wasn't buying it. She had to give him a reason to trust Mitch. To think he'd gotten away with it.

"Darren killed his wife," she blurted out. The hand on her arm squeezed.

Mitch only laughed. "Sure he did."

"And it wasn't Robby. Darren raped all those women."

His smile never wavered. "Christ, lady, how stupid do I look? You want to cuff her, Darren, or can I?"

Darren's grip loosened, and she thought they'd done it. She thought he was going to let go of her.

"Nice try, Mitch."

She gasped as Darren yanked her in front of him, shoving the gun against her temple. When she refocused on Mitch, his gun was drawn.

"What tipped you off?" Mitch asked, his eyes not leaving Darren's. He sounded calm, casual even.

"Your car wasn't in the driveway. If you didn't know something was up, why not park where I would see it?"

Mitch shrugged. "It was worth a shot."

"How did you know it was me?"

"The beer. What were you going to do? Wait till I passed out then break in and take her?"

"Something like that."

"Let her go."

"I'm sorry." He pressed the gun deeper into her skin. "I can't do that."

"Is it true? Did you rape those women? Is that why you killed Diane? She found out?"

"It was her own fault. She had to go sticking her nose into my business. You know what she was like. So damned bossy."

"You sent an innocent man to jail."

"Innocent?" he scoffed. "He was a sexual deviant. He exposed himself to kids. He deserved to go to jail."

"You brutally raped five women."

He didn't seem to get the connection. He really was nuts. "You should be thanking me."

"Thanking you?"

"I handed you that arrest. I made you a hero. I take care of you."

"Lower your weapon, Darren."

"I can't do that."

"The entire Lincoln police department is waiting for you outside. You're not going anywhere. Turn yourself in."

Darren's voice lost that cocky edge. "I'm not going to jail. You know what happens to cops in prison."

"I'll make sure you're taken care of. I owe you, right?" He raised his gun, aiming for Darren's head. "I will shoot you."

"If that's the way it has to be." His voice was eerily calm. "I shoot her, you shoot me. Sounds fair to me."

He would, too. Jill knew that if she was going to make it out of this alive, she had to do something. It was now or never. If she could figure out a way to signal Mitch, she could shove Darren's arm away and give him a shot, but his eyes hadn't wavered from Darren. It was as if he was deliberately not looking at her.

"I love you, Mitch," she said.

He looked at her. He finally met her eyes. She held three fingers to her chest, lowered her eyes so he would follow her gaze. His eyes flickered down for an instant.

He knew what she wanted him to do. He gave the slightest shake of his head. "No."

Behind her she could feel Darren tensing. Her back was soaked with his perspiration.

"Yes, I do," she said.

"This is your last chance to tell her you love her, Mitch."

She mouthed the words "on the count of three" and saw Mitch's hand tighten around his gun. Just like she'd said the other day. He gets me, you get him. Though she'd never expected it to end like this.

One. She curled one finger in.

"I love you," he said.

Two. She curled another.

"I love you, too."

Three—

She shoved up hard with one hand, pushing Darren's arm up, and the gun away from her. She heard one shot ring out, and another blast right behind her, then felt a splitting pain in her shoulder.

Then everything went black.

As the room filled with police, Mitch knelt next to Jill, keeping pressure on her shoulder. There was so much blood. He felt weak-kneed and dizzy. He'd never been bothered by the sight of it, but it was a different story when it was all over the woman he loved.

Without a doubt, she was one of the bravest people he'd ever known, and every bit of love he felt for her welled up, choking him. If he could have just one more chance…

"The ambulance is one minute out, Detective."

He glanced over and saw an officer checking Darren for a pulse. "Is he dead?"

The officer nodded. "Sounds like you didn't have a choice."

"Did they get it all on tape?"

"Every word."

Mitch reached into his shirt and ripped the wire from his chest. They'd solved five rapes, two attacks and one murder today. Darren was a one-man crime wave. "What about her husband?"

"We're holding him."

"Did he have anything to say?"

"Actually, he seemed pretty eager to cooperate. I think he has an idea that he could be in a lot of trouble."

"What did he say—was he in on it with Darren?"

"He told us he got an anonymous call saying his wife had been located. He was given instructions where to fly to, what hotel to stay in. From what I understand, it was the hotel where you guys were supposed to be keeping her tonight."

"So it *was* Darren that called him? He planned to…" He couldn't even make himself say the words.

"Only thing is, when Mr. Stone got to the hotel, there was a message saying the plan had changed and they were supposed to meet here at the house."

"Did Mr. Stone tell you what he planned to do when he got his hands on her? Was that a part of their plan?"

"He swears he only wanted to talk to her. He's been under suspicion for her disappearance. He said he wanted to clear his name. You're welcome to question him."

"How about I let you handle it. Put me in a room with that guy and I'm likely to rip him apart."

"No problem, Detective."

"Mitch?"

Mitch looked down. Jill's eyes were open.

"Did we get him?" she asked weakly.

"We got him."

She winced. "It hurts."

"Hang on, you hear me? The ambulance is almost here." He could hear them pulling up. He looked down at the blood soaking her shirt and covering his hands.

He sucked in several deep breaths. He had to hold it together. He had to stay strong for Jill's sake.

"Is Darren…"

"He's dead, honey. He can't hurt you anymore. He can't hurt anyone."

She reached up and touched his arm. "I'm so sorry. He was your friend."

Christ, she was lying there bleeding to death and she was worried about him. Tears burned his eyes. He could not lose her.

She sighed and closed her eyes. "Stay with me?"

"I'm not going anywhere."

EMS workers entered the house with a gurney and Mitch had to get out of the way. They evaluated her, and within minutes had her in the back of the ambulance. Mitch climbed in with her. There was no way he was going to leave her, not after he'd told her he'd stay with her. If he hadn't left her in the first place none of this would have happened. He would never forgive himself for being so stubborn.

As he sat down beside her, Jill held out her hand. He took it and gently pressed a kiss to the back of it. She closed her eyes, wincing with every bump as the ambulance swung out onto the main road. But in typical Jill fashion, she didn't utter a word of complaint. Mitch gripped her hand, wishing he could absorb her pain.

"Can you give her anything?" he asked the paramedic taking her blood pressure.

She shook her head. "She's lost too much blood. Her pressure's low."

"How far are we from the hospital?"

"Seven minutes."

Seven minutes that would feel like a lifetime. Seven minutes that could be a minute too long.

"I thought I would never see you again." Tears leaked from the corners of Jill's eyes. "Then you would never know how much I love you."

"I love you, too."

She was the woman he was meant to spend the rest of his life with. It didn't matter anymore what side of the law either stood on, or what adversity they might face. They would make it work.

He didn't want to think about the alternative.

Chapter 18

Mitch shifted uncomfortably, leaning his head against the wall. Though the chair in Jane's hospital room was padded, it wasn't exactly conducive to a restful night's sleep. Looking up through half-closed eyes, he shaded his face from the sunshine pouring in the window above him. From the looks of it, the night was over. The nurses had urged him to go home and get some rest, but he wanted to be there in case Jill woke asking for him. He didn't want her to be alone.

She'd spent the better portion of the night in surgery to repair the hole left by the bullet that had ripped through her shoulder. Just the thought of what she'd endured sent a deep shudder through him. When they'd wheeled her away, he wasn't sure if he would ever see her alive again.

He heard a soft rustling across the room and bolted up from his seat. Jill's eyes were open. She'd uttered a few groggy and incoherent words after her surgery but hadn't roused all night. Now she looked alert and coherent.

"How long have you been awake?" he asked.

"Not long." Her voice was rough from sleep, but sounded strong. She was going to be okay.

He sat next to her on the bed, cautiously taking her hand, afraid he might hurt her. "You know, we've really got to stop meeting this way."

She gazed around the room, looking confused. "Where am I?"

"In Pontiac. It was the closest hospital."

"Hospital?"

He realized she must still be groggy from the pain medication they'd given her. "You were shot, Jill. Remember last night?"

"Jill?"

"Yeah, that's your real name, remember?"

She pulled her hand free, brow furrowing. "Do I know you?"

"That's not funny." When she didn't laugh or so much as crack a smile, his heart slammed hard against his rib cage. Oh, no, not again. "You're not kidding, are you? You really don't remember?"

She looked up at him, eyes wide and frightened, then a slow grin spread across her face. "Gotcha."

He shook his head, so relieved he felt like crying. "Christ, don't scare me like that."

Jill laughed, then winced in pain. "You should have seen the look on your face. It was priceless."

"Don't ever do that to me again." He took her hand, kissing it gently. This was definitely his "Jane." "I guess it's safe to assume you're feeling okay?"

"Still a little fuzzy, and every inch of me hurts. I've really made a mess of things this time, haven't I?"

"This wasn't your fault."

She laid a hand on his arm, eyes full of sympathy. "I'm sorry, Mitch. Despite everything he's done, he was your friend for a long time. It still has to hurt."

Part of him wanted to feel bad for Darren. The Darren who had been his best friend. But their friendship had been a lie, and Mitch wasn't sure if he could ever forgive that. All he could do now was see that Darren's kids were taken care of. "It's probably better this way. Cops don't do well in prison."

"David, my husband, did he—"

"He's in custody, but Greene said they'll probably be releasing him today. He claims he only came here so he could clear his name. The police have no proof otherwise."

"What if he comes here, to the hospital?"

The mere idea sent Mitch's hackles up. "He'll have to get through me first. He comes within ten miles of you, I'll break every bone in his body."

Smiling, she reached up and cupped his cheek. "I appreciate the gesture, but if anyone is going to be kicking his ass around here, it'll be me."

He leaned into her hand, loved that he was feeling her touch again. That, if he had his way, he would be feeling it for the rest of his life. "I won't let him hurt you again."

"I'm not afraid anymore. Without fear, David has no power over me."

"He called your parents. All this time they thought you were dead. They're on their way here. Their flight is due in this afternoon."

"I'm not sure I'm ready to see them. It's been so long."

"I told the hospital staff, no visitors until you're ready." Mitch brushed her hair from her face, searching her eyes. "If I'd only driven you home myself last night. If I hadn't been so stubborn—"

"If I had just approached you that first night outside the station, none of this would have happened. We could drive ourselves crazy with what-ifs. Let's just be grateful we're okay. Relatively speaking."

"You said before that if we had met under different circumstances, our standing on different sides of the law would have prevented us from taking a chance on each other."

"We're still standing on opposite sides."

"And it doesn't matter any more to me now than it would have then. I would have known the instant I looked at you, that you were the one for me. It may have taken me a while to admit it to myself, but I would have. And I don't care what it takes. We'll make this work." Mitch caressed her cheek. He couldn't get enough of just touching her, being close. "If it means switching to a new line of work, then that's what I'll do. I could start a security agency, or become a P.I. I could even go to law school."

"You love being a cop, Mitch."

"But I love you more."

Tears welled in Jill's eyes. That was probably the sweetest thing anyone had ever said to her. Ignoring the pain in her shoulder, she pulled him close, hugging herself to his chest. "I don't think that's going to be necessary. I've been seriously considering going legit."

He pulled back, looked her in the eye. "You don't have to do that for me."

"I'm doing it for *me*. I thought maybe I would go back to school. I could get into therapy or social work. That way I could still help people."

A smile softened his face. "Whatever you want to do, I'm behind you one hundred percent."

She feathered her fingers through his hair, rubbed her palm against his beard-roughened cheek. She ached something fierce from the ends of her hair all the way to her toenails, yet she'd never felt so deeply content. For the first time in her life she felt like someone really understood her, and she was right where she was supposed to be.

"I want to spend hours just talking to you. There's still so much we need to learn about each other. I want you to tell me everything." He gave her one of his heart-stopping grins. "And when you're ready, I want to marry you, and have babies with you. I want it all."

Tears spilled out of her eyes and dribbled down her cheeks. "You're sure you know what you're getting yourself into? You know that honest thing I do. If I think you're acting like an idiot I'm going to tell you so. And if we have a problem I'm going to make you talk it out."

"I wouldn't have it any other way."

"Not only that, but I tried the housewife thing once before. I'd go stir-crazy in a week. I want a career *and* a family."

He nodded. "Absolutely."

"And I need a husband who's willing to help out. He'll have to change diapers and maybe cook dinner a few nights a week if I have to work late."

"We'll split everything fifty-fifty."

She narrowed her eyes at him. "Even if that means buying feminine hygiene products while you're doing the grocery shopping?"

He gave a hearty laugh. "Even that."

"In that case, Detective—" she pressed a firm kiss to his lips, sealing the deal "—you just got yourself a wife."

* * * * *

SILHOUETTE®
Sensation™

EVERYBODY'S HERO
by Karen Templeton

The Men of Mayes County
It was an all-out war between the sexes – and Jo was losing the battle. Would his need to be with Taylor withstand the secret he carried?

MIDNIGHT HERO by Diana Duncan

Forever in a Day
As time ticked down to an explosive detonation, agent Conall O'Rourke and bookstore manager Bailey Chambers worked to save innocent hostages – and themselves.

ALONE IN THE DARK
by Marie Ferrarella

Cavanaugh Justice
Patience Cavanaugh had vowed never to date a cop, but detective Brady Coltrane was the type of man to make her break her own rules…

Don't miss out!
On sale from 18th November 2005

0805/SH/LC125

▼ SILHOUETTE®
Sensation™

is thrilled to introduce the strong and savvy women of

BOMBSHELL

ATHENA ACADEMY

THE PRESSURE IS ON.
THE STAKES ARE LIFE AND DEATH.
WHAT WOULD YOU DO?

Trained together at the Athena Academy, these six women vowed to help each other when in need. Now one of their own has been murdered and it is up to them to find the killer, before they become the next victims…

DOUBLE-CROSS by Meredith Fletcher
August 2005

PURSUED by Catherine Mann
September 2005

JUSTICE by Debra Webb
October 2005

DECEIVED by Carla Cassidy
November 2005

CONTACT by Evelyn Vaughn
December 2005

Make your Christmas wish list – and check it twice! ★

Watch out for these very special holiday stories – all featuring the incomparable charm and romance of the Christmas season.

By Jasmine Cresswell, Tara Taylor
Quinn and Kate Hoffmann
On sale 21st October 2005

By Lynnette Kent and
Sherry Lewis
On sale 21st October 2005

By Lucy Monroe and
Louise Allen
On sale 4th November 2005

By Heather Graham,
Lindsay McKenna, Marilyn
Pappano and Annette Broadrick
On sale 18th November 2005

By Marion Lennox, Josie Metcalfe
and Kate Hardy
On sale 2nd December 2005

By Margaret Moore, Terri Brisbin
and Gail Ranstrom
On sale 2nd December 2005

By Lisa Jackson, Barbara Boswell
and Linda Turner
On sale 18th November 2005

FREE

4 BOOKS AND A SURPRISE GIFT!

We would like to take this opportunity to thank you for reading this Silhouette® book by offering you the chance to take FOUR more specially selected titles from the Sensation™ series absolutely FREE! We're also making this offer to introduce you to the benefits of the Reader Service™—

- ★ **FREE home delivery**
- ★ **FREE gifts and competitions**
- ★ **FREE monthly Newsletter**
- ★ **Books available before they're in the shops**
- ★ **Exclusive Reader Service offers**

Accepting these FREE books and gift places you under no obligation to buy; you may cancel at any time, even after receiving your free shipment. Simply complete your details below and return the entire page to the address below. You don't even need a stamp!

YES! Please send me 4 free Sensation books and a surprise gift. I understand that unless you hear from me, I will receive 6 superb new titles every month for just £3.05 each, postage and packing free. I am under no obligation to purchase any books and may cancel my subscription at any time. The free books and gift will be mine to keep in any case.

S5ZEE

Ms/Mrs/Miss/Mr...Initials ....
                                                                          BLOCK CAPITALS PLEASE

Surname ....

Address ....

....

....Postcode ....

Send this whole page to:
The Reader Service, FREEPOST CN81, Croydon, CR9 3WZ